Sov

MAN RIDING WEST

c

MAN RIDING WEST
A Western Sextet

LOUIS L'AMOUR
Edited by
JON TUSKA

SAGEBRUSH
Large Print Westerns

First published in Great Britain by ISIS Publishing Ltd.
First published in the United States by ISIS Publishing Ltd.

Published in Large Print 2014 by ISIS Publishing Ltd.,
7 Centremead, Osney Mead, Oxford OX2 0ES
by arrangement with
Golden West Literary Agency

CIP data is available for this title from the British Library

ISBN 978–0–7531–5351–2 (pb)

Printed and bound in Great Britain by
T. J. International Ltd., Padstow, Cornwall

Table of Contents

Introduction

by Jon Tuska

Louis Dearborn LaMoore (1908–1988) was born in Jamestown, North Dakota. He left home at fifteen and subsequently held a wide variety of jobs although he worked mostly as a merchant seaman. From his earliest youth, L'Amour had a love of verse. His first published work was a poem, "The Chap Worth While", appearing when he was eighteen years old in his former hometown's newspaper, the *Jamestown Sun*. It is the only poem from his early years that he left out of *Smoke From This Altar*, which appeared in 1939 from Lusk Publishers in Oklahoma City, a book which L'Amour published himself; however, this poem is reproduced in *The Louis L'Amour Companion* (Andrews and McMeel, 1992) edited by Robert Weinberg. L'Amour wrote poems and articles for a number of small circulation arts magazines all through the early 1930s and, after hundreds of rejection slips, finally had his first story accepted, "Anything for a Pal" in *True Gang Life* (10/35). He returned in 1938 to live with his family where they had settled in Choctaw, Oklahoma, determined to make writing his career. He

1

wrote a fight story bought by Standard Magazines that year and became acquainted with editor Leo Margulies who was to play an important role later in L'Amour's life. "The Town No Guns Could Tame" in *New Western* (3/40) was his first published Western story.

During the Second World War L'Amour was drafted and ultimately served with the U.S. Army Transportation Corps in Europe. However, in the two years before he was shipped out, he managed to write a great many adventure stories for Standard Magazines. The first story he published in 1946, the year of his discharge, was a Western, "Law of the Desert Born" in *Dime Western* (4/46). A call to Leo Margulies resulted in L'Amour's agreeing to write Western stories for the various Western pulp magazines published by Standard Magazines, a third of which appeared under the byline Jim Mayo, the name of a character in L'Amour's earlier adventure fiction. The proposal for L'Amour to write new Hopalong Cassidy novels came from Margulies who wanted to launch *Hopalong Cassidy's Western Magazine* to take advantage of the popularity William Boyd's old films and new television series were enjoying with a new generation. Doubleday & Company agreed to publish the pulp novelettes in hard cover books. L'Amour was paid $500 a story, no royalties, and he was assigned the house name Tex Burns. L'Amour read Clarence E. Mulford's books about the Bar-20 and based his Hopalong Cassidy on Mulford's original creation. Only two issues of the magazine appeared before it ceased publication. Doubleday felt that the Hopalong character had to appear exactly as William

Boyd did in the films and on television and thus even the first two novels had to be revamped to meet with this requirement prior to publication in book form.

L'Amour's first Western novel under his own byline was *Westward The Tide* (World's Work, 1950). It was rejected by every American publisher to which it was submitted. World's Work paid a flat £75 without royalties for British Empire rights in perpetuity. L'Amour sold his first Western short story to a slick magazine a year later, "The Gift of Cochise" in *Collier's* (7/5/52). Robert Fellows and John Wayne purchased screen rights to this story from L'Amour for $4,000 and James Edward Grant, one of Wayne's favorite screenwriters, developed a script from it, changing L'Amour's Ches Lane to Hondo Lane. L'Amour retained the right to novelize Grant's screenplay, which differs substantially from his short story, and he was able to get an endorsement from Wayne to be used as a blurb, stating that *Hondo* was the finest Western Wayne had ever read. *Hondo* (Fawcett Gold Medal, 1953) by Louis L'Amour was released on the same day as the film, *Hondo* (Warner, 1953), with a first printing of 320,000 copies.

With *Showdown At Yellow Butte* (Ace, 1953) by Jim Mayo, L'Amour began a series of short Western novels for Don Wollheim that could be doubled with other short novels by other authors in Ace Publishing's paperback two-fers. Advances on these were $800 and usually the author never earned any royalties. *Heller With A Gun* (Fawcett Gold Medal, 1955) was the first of a series of original Westerns L'Amour had agreed to write under his own name following the success for Fawcett of *Hondo*. L'Amour wanted even this early to have his Western novels published in hard cover editions. He expanded "Guns of the Timberland" by Jim Mayo in *West* (9/50) for *Guns Of The Timberlands* (Jason Press, 1955), a hard cover Western for which he was paid an advance of $250. Another novel for Jason Press followed and then *Silver Canyon* (Avalon Books, 1956) for Thomas Bouregy & Company. These were basically lending library publishers and the books seldom earned much money above the small advances paid.

The great turn in L'Amour's fortunes came about because of problems Saul David was having with his original paperback Westerns program at Bantam Books. Fred Glidden had been signed to a contract to produce two original paperback Luke Short Western novels a year for an advance of $15,000 each. It was a long-term contract but, in the first ten years of it, Fred only wrote six novels. Literary agent Marguerite Harper then persuaded Bantam that Fred's brother, Jon, could help fulfill the contract and Jon was signed for eight Peter Dawson Western novels. When Jon died suddenly before completing even one book for Bantam, Harper managed to engage a ghost writer at the Disney studios to write these eight "Peter Dawson" novels, beginning with *The Savages* (Bantam, 1959). They proved inferior to anything Jon had ever written and what sales they had seemed to be due only to the Peter Dawson name.

Saul David wanted to know from L'Amour if *he* could deliver two Western novels a year. L'Amour said he could, and he did. In fact, by 1962 this number was increased to three original paperback novels a year. The first L'Amour novel to appear under the Bantam contract was *Radigan* (Bantam, 1958). It seemed to me after I read all of the Western stories L'Amour ever wrote in preparation for my essay, "Louis L'Amour's Western Fiction" in *A Variable Harvest* (McFarland, 1990), that by the time L'Amour wrote "Riders of the Dawn" in *Giant Western* (6/51), the short novel he later expanded to form *Silver Canyon*, that he had almost burned out on the Western story, and this was years before his fame, wealth, and tremendous sales figures. He had developed seven basic plot situations in his pulp Western stories and he used them over and over again in writing his original paperback Westerns. FLINT (Bantam, 1960), considered by many to be one of L'Amour's better efforts, is basically a reprise of the range war plot which, of the seven, is the one L'Amour used most often. L'Amour's hero, Flint, knows about a hide-out in the badlands (where, depending on the story, something is hidden: cattle, horses, outlaws, etc.). Even certain episodes within his basic plots are repeated again and again. Flint scales a sharp V in a cañon wall to escape a tight spot as Jim Gatlin had before him in L'Amour's "The Black Rock Coffin Makers" in *.44 Western* (2/50) and many a L'Amour hero would again.

Basic to this range war plot is the villain's means for crowding out the other ranchers in a district. He brings in a giant herd that requires all the available grass and forces all the smaller ranchers out of business. It was this same strategy Bantam used in marketing L'Amour. *All* of his Western titles were continuously kept in print. Independent distributors were required to buy titles in lots of 10,000 copies if they wanted access to other Bantam titles at significantly discounted prices. In time L'Amour's paperbacks forced almost every one else off the racks in the Western sections. L'Amour himself comprised the other half of this successful strategy. He dressed up in cowboy outfits, traveled about the country in a motor home visiting with independent distributors, taking them to dinner and charming them, making them personal friends. He promoted himself at every available opportunity. L'Amour insisted that he was telling the stories of the people who had made America a great nation and he appealed to patriotism as much as to commercialism in his rhetoric.

His fiction suffered, of course, stories written hurriedly and submitted in their first draft and published as he wrote them. A character would have a rifle in his hand, a model not yet invented in the period in which the story was set, and when he crossed a street the rifle would vanish without explanation. A scene would begin in a saloon and suddenly the setting would be a hotel dining room. Characters would die once and, a few pages later, die again. An old man for most of a story would turn out to be in his twenties.

Once when we were talking and Louis had showed me his topographical maps and his library of thousands of volumes which he claimed he used for research, he asserted that, if he claimed there was a rock in a road at a certain point in a story, his readers knew that if they

6

went to that spot they would find the rock just as he described it. I told him that might be so but I personally was troubled by the many inconsistencies in his stories. Take *Last Stand At Papago Wells* (Fawcett Gold Medal, 1957). Five characters are killed during an Indian raid. One of the surviving characters emerges from seclusion after the attack and counts six corpses.

"I'll have to go back and count them again," L'Amour said, and smiled. "But, you know, I don't think the people who read my books would really care."

All of this notwithstanding, there are many fine, and some spectacular, moments in Louis L'Amour's Western fiction. I think he was at his best in the shorter forms, especially his magazine stories, and the two best stories he ever wrote appeared in the 1950s, "The Gift of Cochise" early in the decade and "War Party" in *The Saturday Evening Post* (6/59). The latter was later expanded by L'Amour to serve as the opening chapters for *Bendigo Shafter* (Dutton, 1979). That book is so poorly structured that Harold Kuebler, senior editor at Doubleday & Company to whom it was first offered, said he would not publish it unless L'Amour undertook extensive revisions. This L'Amour refused to do and, eventually, Bantam started a hard cover publishing program to accommodate him when no other hard cover publisher proved willing to accept his books as he wrote them. Yet "War Party" possesses several of the characteristics in purest form which I suspect, no matter how diluted they ultimately would become, account in largest measure for the loyal following Louis L'Amour won from his readers: the young male narrator who is in the process of growing into manhood and who is evaluating other human beings and his own experiences; a resourceful frontier woman who has beauty as well as fortitude; a strong male character who is single and hence marriageable; and the powerful, romantic, strangely compelling vision of the American West which invests L'Amour's Western fiction and makes it such a delightful escape from the cares of a later time — in this author's words from this story, that "big country needing big men and women to live in it" and where there was no place for "the frightened or the mean."

His Brother's Debt

"You're yellow, Casady!" Ben Kerr shouted. "Yellow as saffron! You ain't got the guts of a coyote! Draw, damn you. Fill your hand so I can kill you! You ain't fit to live!" Kerr stepped forward, his big hands spread over his gun butts. "Go ahead, reach!"

Rock Casady, numb with fear, stepped slowly back, his face gray. To right and left were the amazed and incredulous faces of his friends, the men he had ridden with on the O Bar, staring, unbelieving.

Sweat broke out on his face. He felt his stomach retch and twist within him. Turning suddenly, he plunged blindly through the door and fled.

Behind him, one by one, his shamefaced, unbelieving friends from the O Bar slowly sifted from the crowd. Heads hanging, they headed homeward. Rock Casady was yellow. The man they had worked with, sweated with, laughed with. The last man they would have suspected. Yellow.

Westward, with the wind in his face and tears burning his eyes, his horse's hoofs beating out a mad tattoo upon the hard trail, fled Rock Casady, alone in the darkness.

Nor did he stop. Avoiding towns and holding to the hills, he rode steadily westward. There were days when he starved and days when he found game, a quail or two, killed with unerring shots from a six-gun that never seemed to miss. Once he shot a deer. He rode wide of towns and deliberately erased his trail, although he knew no one was following him or cared where he went.

Four months later, leaner, unshaven, and saddle-weary, he rode into the yard of the Three Spoke Wheel. Foreman Tom Bell saw him coming and glanced around at his boss, big Frank Stockman.

"Look what's comin'. Looks like he's lived in the hills. On the dodge, maybe."

"Huntin' grub, most likely. He's a strappin' big man, though, an' looks like a hand. Better ask him if he wants a job. With Pete Vorys around, we'll have to be huntin' strangers or we'll be out of help."

The mirror on the wall of the bunkhouse was neither cracked nor marred, but Rock Casady could almost wish that it was. Bathed and shaved, he looked into the tortured eyes of a dark, attractive young man with wavy hair and a strong jaw.

People had told him many times that he was a handsome man, but when he looked into his eyes, he knew he looked into the eyes of a coward. He had a yellow streak. The first time — well, the first time but one — that he had faced a man with a gun he had backed down cold. He had run like a baby. He had shown the white feather.

Tall, strongly built, skillful with rope or horse, knowing with stock, he was a top hand in any outfit. An outright genius with guns, men had often said they would hate to face him in a shoot-out. He had worked hard and played rough, getting the most out of life until that day in the saloon in El Paso when Ben Kerr, gunman and cattle rustler, gambler and bully, had called him, and he had backed down.

Tom Bell was a knowing and kindly man. Aware that something was riding Casady, he told him his job and left him alone. Stockman watched him top off a bad bronco on the first morning and glanced at Bell.

"If he does everything like he rides, we've got us a hand."

And Casady did everything as well. A week after he had hired out, he was doing as much work as any two men. And the jobs they avoided, the lonely jobs, he accepted eagerly.

"Notice something else?" Stockman asked the ranch owner one morning. "That new hand sure likes the jobs that keep him away from the ranch."

Stockman nodded. "Away from people. It ain't natural, Tom. He ain't been to Three Lakes once since he's been here."

Sue Landon looked up at her uncle. "Maybe he's broke!" she exclaimed. "No cowhand could have fun in town when he's broke."

Bell shook his head. "It ain't that, Sue. He had money when he first come in here. I saw it. He had anyway two hundred dollars, and for a forty-a-month cowpoke that's a lot of money."

"Notice something else?" Stockman asked. "He never packs a gun. Only man on the ranch who doesn't. You'd better warn him about Pete Vorys."

"I did." Bell frowned. "I can't figure this *hombre*, boss. I did warn him, and that was the very day he began askin' for all the bad jobs. Why, he's the only man on the place who'll fetch grub to Cat McLeod without bein' bullied into it."

"Over in that Rock Cañon country?" Stockman smiled. "That's a rough ride for any man. I don't blame the boys, but you've got to hand it to old Cat. He's killed nine lions and forty-two coyotes in the past ninety days. If he keeps that up, we won't have so much stock lost."

"Too bad he ain't just as good on rustlers. Maybe — " Bell grinned " — we ought to turn him loose on Pete Vorys."

Rock Casady kept his Appaloosa gelding moving steadily. The two pack horses ambled placidly behind, seemingly content to be away from the ranch. The old restlessness was coming back to Casady, and he had been on the Three Spoke only a few weeks. He knew they liked him, knew that despite his taciturn manner and desire to be alone, the hands liked him as well as did Stockman or Bell.

He did his work and more, and he was a hand. He avoided poker games that might lead to trouble and stayed away from town. He was anxiously figuring some way to be absent from the ranch on the following Saturday, for he knew the whole crowd was going to a dance and shindig in Three Lakes.

While he talked little, he heard much. He was aware of impending trouble between the Three Spoke Wheel outfit and the gang of Pete Vorys. The latter, who seemed to ride the country as he pleased, owned a small ranch north of Three Lakes, near town. He had a dozen tough hands and usually spent money freely. All his hands had money, and, while no one dared say it, all knew he was rustling.

Yet he was not the ringleader. Behind him there was someone else, someone who had only recently become involved, for recently there had been a change. Larger bunches of cattle were being stolen, and more care was taken to leave no trail. The carelessness of Vorys had given way to shrewder operation, and Casady overheard enough talk to know that Stockman believed a new brain was directing the rustling.

He heard much of Pete Vorys. He was a big man, bigger than Rock. He was a killer with at least seven notches on his gun. He was pugnacious and quarrelsome, itching for a fight with gun or fists. He had, only a few weeks before, whipped Sandy Kane, a Three Spoke hand, within an inch of his life. He was bold, domineering, and tough.

The hands on the Three Spoke were good men. They were hard workers, willing to fight, but not one of them was good enough to tackle Vorys with either fists or gun.

Cat McLeod was scraping a hide when Rock rode into his camp in Blue Spring Valley. He got up, wiping his hands on his jeans and grinning.

"Howdy, son. You sure are a sight for sore eyes. It ain't no use quibblin', I sure get my grub on time when you're on that ranch. Hope you stay."

Rock swung down. He liked the valley and liked Cat. "Maybe I'll pull out, Cat." He looked around. "I might even come up here to stay. I like it."

McLeod glanced at him out of the corners of his eyes. "Glad to have you, son. This sure ain't no country for a young feller, though. It's a huntin' an' fishin' country, but no women here, an' no likker. Nothin' much to do, all said an' done."

Casady unsaddled in silence. It was better, though, than a run-in with Vorys, he thought. At least, nobody here knew he was yellow. They liked him and he was one of them, but he was careful.

"Ain't more trouble down below, is there? That Vorys cuttin' up much?" The old man noted the gun Rock was wearing for the trip.

"Some. I hear the boys talkin' about him."

"Never seen him yourself?" Cat asked quizzically. "I been thinkin' ever since you come up here, son. Might be a good thing for this country if you did have trouble with Vorys. You're nigh as big as him, an' you move like a catamount. An' me, I know 'em. Never seen a man lighter on his feet than you."

"Not me," Rock spoke stiffly. "I'm a peace-lovin' man, Cat. I want no trouble with anybody."

McLeod studied the matter as he worked over his hide. For a long time now he had known something was bothering Rock Casady. Perhaps this last remark, that he wanted no trouble with anybody, was the answer?

Cat McLeod was a student of mankind as well as the animals upon which he practiced his trade. In a lifetime of living along the frontier and in the world's far places, he had learned a lot about men who liked to live alone and about men who sought the wilderness. If it was true that Rock wanted no trouble, it certainly was not from lack of ability to handle it.

There had been that time when Cat had fallen, stumbling to hands and knees. Right before him, not three feet from his face and much nearer his outstretched hands, lay one of the biggest rattlers Cat had ever seen. The snake's head jerked back above its coil, and then, with a gun's roar blasting in his ears, that head was gone and the snake was a writhing mass of coils, showing only a bloody stump where the head had been.

Cat had gotten to his feet, gray-faced, and turned. Rock Casady was thumbing a shell into his gun. The young man had grinned.

"That was a close one," he had said cheerfully.

McLeod had dusted off his hands, staring at Casady. "I've heard of men drawin' faster'n a snake could strike, but that's the first time I ever seen it."

Since then he had seen that .44 shoot the heads off quail and he had seen a quick hip shot with the rifle break a deer's neck.

Now his mind reverted to their former topic. "If that Vorys is tied in with some smart *hombre*, there'll be hell to pay. Pete was never no great shakes for brains, but he's tough, tough as all get out. With somebody to think for him, he'll make this country unfit to live in."

Later that night, McLeod looked over his shoulder from the fire. "You know," he said, "if I was wantin' a spread of my own an' didn't care much for folks, like

17

you, I'd go down into the Pleasant Valley Outlet, south of here. Lonely, but she's sure grand country."

Two days later Rock was mending a bridle when Sue Landon walked over to him. She wore jeans and a boy's shirt, and her eyes were bright and lovely.

"Hi!" she said brightly. "You're the new hand? You certainly keep out of the way. All this time on the ranch and I never met you before."

He grinned shyly. "Just a quiet *hombre*, I reckon," he said. "If I had it my way, I'd be over there with Cat all the time."

"Then you won't like the job I have for you," she said. "To ride into Three Lakes with me, riding herd on a couple of pack horses."

"Three Lakes?" He looked up so sharply it startled her. "Into town? I never go into town, ma'am. I don't like the place. Not any town."

"Why, that's silly. Anyway, there's no one else, and Uncle Frank won't let me go alone with Pete Vorys around."

"He wouldn't bother a girl, would he?"

"You sure don't know Pete Vorys," Sue returned grimly. "He does pretty much what he feels like, and everybody's afraid to say anything about it. Although," she added, "with this new partner he's got, he's toned down some. But come on . . . you'll go?"

Reluctantly he got to his feet. She looked at him curiously, not a little piqued. Any other hand on the ranch would have jumped at the chance, and here she had deliberately made sure there were no others available before going to him. Her few distant glimpses

18

of Rock Casady had excited her interest, and she wanted to know him better.

Yet as the trail fell behind them, she had to admit she was getting no place. For shyness there was some excuse, although usually even the most bashful hand lost it when alone with her. Rock Casady was almost sullen, and all she could get out of him were monosyllables.

The truth was that the nearer they drew to Three Lakes, the more worried Rock grew. It had been six months since he had been in a town, and, while it was improbable he would see anyone he knew, there was always a chance. Cowhands were notoriously footloose and fancy-free. Once the story of his backing out of a gunfight got around, he would be through in this country, and he was tired of running.

Yet Three Lakes looked quiet enough as they ambled placidly down the street and tied up in front of the general store. He glanced at Sue tentatively.

"Ma'am," he said, "I'd sure appreciate it if you didn't stay too long. Towns make me nervous."

She looked at him, more than slightly irritated. Her trip with him, so carefully planned, had thus far come to nothing, although she had to admit he was the finest-looking man she had ever seen, and his smile was quick and attractive.

"I won't be long. Why don't you go have a drink? It might do you good!" She said the last sentence a little sharply, and he looked quickly at her, but she was already flouncing into the store, as well as any girl could flounce in jeans.

Slowly he built a cigarette, studying the Hackamore Saloon over the way. He had to admit he was tempted, and probably he was foolish to think that he would get into trouble or that anyone would know him. Nevertheless, he sat down suddenly on the edge of the boardwalk and lighted his smoke.

He was still sitting there when he heard the sound of booted heels on the boardwalk and then heard a raucous voice.

"Hey! Lookit here! One of them no 'count Three Spokers in town. I didn't think any of them had the sand."

In spite of himself, he looked up, knowing instantly that this man was Pete Vorys.

He was broad in the shoulder, with narrow hips. He had a swarthy face with dark, brilliant eyes. That he had been drinking was obvious, but he was far from drunk. With him were two tough-looking hands, both grinning cynically at him.

Vorys was spoiling for a fight. He had never been whipped and doubted there lived a man who could whip him in a tooth-and-nail, knockdown and drag-out battle. This Three Spoker looked big enough to be fun.

"That's a rawhide outfit, anyway," Vorys sneered. "I've a mind to ride out there sometime, just for laughs. Wonder where they hooked this ranny?"

Despite himself, Rock was growing angry. He was not wearing a gun, and Vorys was. He took the cigarette out of his mouth and looked at it. Expecting trouble, a crowd was gathering. He felt his neck growing red.

"Hey, you!" Vorys booted him solidly in the spine, and the kick hurt. At the same time, he slapped Casady with his sombrero. Few things are more calculated to enrage a man.

Rock came to his feet with a lunge. As he turned, with his right palm he grabbed the ankle of Vorys's boot, and with his left fist he smashed him in the stomach, jerking up on the leg. The move was so sudden, so totally unexpected, that there was no chance to spring back. Pete Vorys hit the boardwalk flat on his shoulder blades.

A whoop of delight went up from the crowd, and for an instant Pete Vorys lay stunned. Then with an oath he came off the walk, lunging to his feet.

Rock sprang back, his hands wide. "I'm not packin' a gun!" he yelled.

"I don't need a gun!" Vorys yelled. It was the first time he had ever hit the ground in a fight and he was furious.

He stepped in, driving a left to the head. Rock was no boxer. Indeed, he had rarely fought except in fun. He took that blow now, a stunning wallop on the cheek bone. At the same moment, he let go with a wicked right swing. The punch caught Vorys on the chin and rocked him to his heels.

More astonished than hurt, he sprang in and threw two swings for Rock's chin, and Casady took them both coming in. A tremendous light seemed to burst in his brain, but the next instant he had Pete Vorys in his hands. Grabbing him by the collar and the belt, he heaved him to arm's length overhead and hurled him into the street. Still dazed from the punches he had taken, he sprang after the bigger man, and, seizing him before he could strike more than an ineffectual punch, swung him to arm's length overhead again, and slammed him into the dust.

Four times he grabbed the hapless bully and hurled him to the ground while the crowd whooped and cheered. The last time, his head clearing, he grabbed Vorys's shirt front with his left hand and swung three times into his face, smashing his nose and lips. Then he lifted the man and heaved him into the water tank with such force that water showered around him.

Beside himself, Rock wheeled on the two startled men who had walked with Vorys. Before either could make a move, he grabbed them by their belts. One swung on Rock's face, but he merely ducked his head and heaved. The man's feet flew up and he hit the ground on his back. Promptly Rock stacked the other atop him.

The man started to get up, and Rock swung on his face, knocking him into a sitting position. Then grabbing him, he heaved him into the water tank with Vorys, who was scrambling to get out. Then he dropped the third man into the pool and, putting a hand in Vorys's face, shoved him back.

For an instant, then, while the street rocked with cheers and yells of delight, he stood, panting and staring. Suddenly he was horrified. In his rage he had not thought of what this would mean, but suddenly he knew that they would be hunting him now with guns. He must face a shoot-out or skip the country.

Wheeling, he shoved through the crowd, aware that someone was clinging to his arm. Looking down, he saw Sue beside him. Her eyes were bright with laughter and pride.

"Oh, Rock! That was wonderful. Just wonderful!"

"Let's get out of town," he said quickly. "Now."

So pleased was she by the discomfiture of Pete Vorys and his hands by a Three Spoker that she thought nothing of his haste. His eye swelling and his nose still dripping occasional drops of blood, they hit the trail for the home ranch. All the way, Sue babbled happily over his standing up for the Three Spoke and what it meant, and all the while all he could think of was the fact that on the morrow Vorys would be looking for him with a gun.

He could not face him. It was far better to avoid a fight than to prove himself yellow, and, if he fled the country now, they would never forget what he had done and always make excuses for him. If he stayed behind and showed his yellow streak, he would be ruined.

Frank Stockman was standing on the steps when they rode in. He took one look at Rock's battered face and torn shirt and came off the steps.

"What happened?" he demanded. "Was it that Pete Vorys again?"

Tom Bell and two other hands were walking up from the bunkhouse, staring at Rock. But already, while he stripped the saddles from the horses, Sue Landon was telling the story, and it lost nothing in the telling. Rock Casady of the Three Spoke had not only whipped Pete

23

Vorys soundly, but he had ducked Pete and two of his tough hands in the Three Lakes water tank!

The hands crowded around him, crowing and happy, slapping him on the back and grinning. Sandy Kane gripped his hand.

"Thanks, pardner," he said grimly, "I don't feel so bad now."

Rock smiled weakly, but inside he was sick. It was going to look bad, but he was pulling out. He said nothing, but after supper he got his own horse, threw the saddle aboard, and then rustled his gear. When he was all packed, he drew a deep breath and walked toward the ranch house.

Stockman was sitting on the wide verandah with Bell and Sue. She got up when he drew near, her eyes bright. He avoided her glance, suddenly aware of how much her praise and happiness meant to him. In his weeks on the Three Spoke, while he had never talked to her before today, his eyes had followed her every move.

"How are you, son?" Stockman said jovially. "You've made this a red-letter day on the Three Spoke. Come up an' sit down. Bell was just talking here. He says he needs a *segundo*, an' I reckon he's right. How'd you like the job? Eighty a month?"

He swallowed. "Sorry, boss. I got to be movin'. I want my time."

"You what?" Bell took his pipe from his mouth and stared.

"I got to roll my hoop," he said stiffly. "I don't want trouble."

Frank Stockman came quickly to his feet. "But listen, man," he protested. "You've just whipped the best man around this country. You've made a place for yourself here. The boys think you're great. So do I. So does Tom. As for Sue here, all she's done is talk about how wonderful you are. Why, son, you came in here a drifter, an' now you've made a place for yourself. Stick around. We need men like you."

Despite himself, Casady was wavering. This was what he had always wanted, and wanted now, since the bleak months of his lonely riding, more than ever. A place where he was at home, men who liked him, and a girl . . .

"Stay on," Stockman said more quietly. "You can handle any trouble that comes, and I promise you, the Three Spoke will back any play you make. Why, with you to head 'em, we can run Pete Vorys and that slick partner of his, that Ben Kerr, clean out of the country."

Casady's face blanched. "Who? Did you say, Ben Kerr?"

"Why, sure." Stockman stared at him curiously, aware of the shocked expression on Rock's face. "Ben Kerr's the *hombre* who come in here to side Vorys. He's the smart one who's puttin' all those fancy ideas in Pete's head. He's a brother-in-law of Vorys's or something."

Ben Kerr — here! That settled it. He could not stay now. There was no time to stay. His mind leaped ahead. Vorys would tell his story, of course. His name would be mentioned, or, if not his name, his description. Kerr would know, and he wouldn't waste time. Why, even now . . .

"Give me my money," Casady said sharply. "I'm movin' out right now. Thanks for all you've offered, but I'm riding. I want no trouble."

Stockman's face stiffened. "Why, sure," he said, "if you feel that way about it." He took a roll of bills from his pocket and coolly paid over the money, then abruptly he turned his back and walked inside.

Casady wheeled, his heart sick within him, and started for the corral. He heard running steps behind him, and then a light touch on his arm. He looked down, his eyes miserable, into Sue's face.

"Don't go, Rock," she pleaded gently. "Please don't go. We all want you to stay."

He shook his head. "I can't, Sue. I can't stay. I want no gun trouble."

There — it was out.

She stepped back, and slowly her face changed. Girl that she was, she still had grown up in the tradition of the West. A man fought his battles with gun or fist; he did not run away.

"Oh?" Her amazed contempt cut him like a whip. "So that's it? You're afraid to face a gun? Afraid for your life?" She stared at him. "Why, Rock Casady," her voice lifted as realization broke over her, "you're yellow!"

Hours later, far back in the darkness of night in the mountains, her words rang in his ears. She had called him yellow! She had called him a coward!

Rock Casady, sick at heart, rode slowly into the darkness. At first he rode with no thought but to

26

escape, and then, as his awareness began to return, he studied the situation. Lee's Ferry was northeast, and to the south he was bottled by the Colorado Cañon. North it was mostly Vorys's range, and west lay Three Lakes and the trails leading to it. East, the cañons fenced him off, also, but east lay a lonely, little-known country, ridden only by Cat McLeod in his wanderings after varmints that preyed upon Three Spoke cattle. In that wilderness he might find some place to hole up. Cat still had plenty of supplies, and he could borrow some from him. Suddenly he remembered the cañon Cat had mentioned, the Pleasant Valley Outlet.

He would not go near Cat. There was game enough, and he had packed away a few things in the grub line when he had rolled his soogan. He found an intermittent stream that trailed down a ravine toward Kane Cañon, and followed it. Pleasant Valley Outlet was not far south of Kane. It would be a good hide-out. After a few weeks, when the excitement was over, he could slip out of the country.

In a lonely cañon that opened from the south wall into Pleasant Valley Cañon, he found a green and lovely spot. There was plenty of driftwood and a cave hollowed from the Kaibab sandstone by wind and water. There he settled clown. Days passed into weeks, and he lived on wild game, berries, and fish. Yet his mind kept turning northwestward toward the Three Spoke, and his thoughts gave him no rest.

On an evening almost three weeks after his escape from the Three Spoke, he was putting his coffee on when he heard a slight sound. Looking up, he saw old Cat McLeod grinning at him.

"Howdy, son." He chuckled. "When you head for the tall timber, you sure do a job of it. My land, I thought I'd never find you. No more trailin' trout swimmin' upstream."

Rock arose stiffly. "Howdy, Cat. Just put the coffee on." He averted his eyes and went about the business of preparing a meal.

Cat seated himself, seemingly unhurried and undisturbed by his scant welcome. He got out his pipe and stuffed it full of tobacco. He talked calmly and quietly about game and fish and the mountain trails.

"Old Mormon crossin' not far from here," he said. "I could show you where it is."

After they had eaten, McLeod leaned back against a rock. "Lots of trouble back at the Three Spoke. I reckon you was the smart one, pullin' out when you did."

Casady made no response, so McLeod continued. "Pete Vorys was some beat up. Two busted ribs, busted nose, some teeth gone. Feller name of Ben Kerr came out to the Three Spoke, huntin' you. Said you was a yella dog an' he knowed you of old. He laughed when he said that, an' said the whole Three Spoke outfit was yella. Stockman, he wouldn't take that, so he went for his gun. Kerr shot him."

Rock's head came up with a jerk. "Shot Stockman? He killed him?" There was horror in his voice. This was his fault — his!

"No, he ain't dead. He's sure bad off, though. Kerr added injury to insult by runnin' off a couple of hundred head of Three Spoke stock. Shot one hand doin' it."

A long silence followed in which the two men smoked moodily. Finally Cat looked across the fire at Rock.

"Son, there's more'n one kind of courage, I say. I seen many a dog stand up to a grizzly that would hightail it from a skunk. Back yonder they say you're yella. Me, I don't figure it so."

"Thanks, Cat," Rock replied simply, miserably. "Thanks a lot, but you're wrong. I am yellow."

"Reckon it takes pretty much of a man to say that, son. But from what I hear, you sure didn't act it against Pete an' his riders. You walloped the tar out of them."

"With my hands it's different. It's . . . it's . . . guns."

McLeod was silent. He poked a twig into the fire and re-lit his pipe.

"Ever kill a man, son?" His eyes probed Rock's, and he saw the young rider's head nod slowly. "Who was it? How'd it happen?"

"It was . . ." He looked up, his face drawn and pale. "I killed my brother, Cat."

McLeod was shocked. His old eyes went wide. "You killed your brother? Your own brother?"

Rock Casady nodded. "Yeah," he said bitterly, "my own brother. The one person in this world that really mattered to me."

Cat stared, and then slowly his brow puckered. "Son," he said, "why don't you tell me about it? Get it out of your system, like."

For a long while Rock was silent. Then he started to speak.

"It was down in Texas. We had a little spread down there, Jack and me. He was only a shade older, but always protecting me, although I sure didn't need it. The finest man who ever walked, he was. Well, we had us a mite of trouble, and this here Ben Kerr was the ringleader. I had trouble with Ben, and he swore to shoot me on sight. I was a hand with a gun, like you know, and I was ready enough to fight, them days. One of the hands told me, and without a word to Jack I lit into the saddle and headed for town.

"Kerr was a gunslick, but I wasn't worried. I knew that I didn't have scarcely a friend in town and that his whole outfit would be there. It was me against them, and I went into town with two guns and sure enough on the prod.

"It was getting late when I hit town. A man I knew told me Ben was around with his outfit and that nobody was going to back me one bit, them all being scared of Ben's boys. He told me, too, that Ben Kerr would shoot me in the back as soon as not, him being that kind.

"I went hunting him. Kid-like, and never in a gunfight before, I was jumpy, mighty jumpy. The light was bad. All of a sudden, I saw one of Ben's boys step out of a door ahead of me. He called out . . . 'Here he is, Ben! Take him!' Then I heard running feet behind

30

me, heard 'em slide to a halt, and I wheeled, drawing as I turned, and fired." His voice sank to a whisper.

Cat, leaning forward, said: "You shot? An' then . . . ?"

"It was Jack. It was my own brother. He'd heard I was in town alone, and he come running to back me up. I drilled him dead center."

Cat McLeod stared up at the young man, utterly appalled. In his kindly old heart he could only guess at the horror that must have filled Casady, then scarcely more than a boy, when he had looked down into that still, dead face and seen his brother.

"Gosh, son." He shook his head in amazed sympathy. "It ain't no wonder you hate gunfights. It sure ain't. But . . . ?" He scowled. "I still don't see . . ." His voice trailed away.

Rock drew a deep breath. "I sold out then and left the country. Went to riding for an outfit near El Paso. One night I come into town with the other hands, and who do I run into but Ben Kerr? He thought I'd run because I was afraid of him, and he got tough. He called me . . . right in front of the outfit. I was going to draw, but all I could see there in front of me was Jack, with that blue hole between his eyes. I turned and ran."

Cat McLeod stared at Rock, and then into the fire. It was no wonder, he reflected. He probably would have run, too. If Rock had drawn, he would have been firing on the image of the brother. It would have been like killing him over again.

"Son," he said slowly, "I know how you feel, but stop a minute an' think about Jack, this brother of yours. He always protected you, you say. He always stood up for you. Now don't you suppose he'd understand? You thought you was all alone in that town. You'd every right in the world to think that was Ben Kerr behind you. I would have thought so, an' I wouldn't have wasted no time shootin', neither.

"You can't run away from yourself. You can't run no farther. Someday you got to stand an' face it, an' it might as well be now. Look at it like this. Would your brother want you livin' like this? Hunted an' scared? He sure wouldn't. Son, ever' man has to pay his own debt an' live his own life. Nobody can do it for you, but, if I was you, I'd sort of figure my brother was dead because of Ben Kerr, an' I'd stop runnin'!"

Rock looked up slowly. "Yeah," he agreed, "I see that plain. But what if when I stepped out to meet him, I look up an' see Jack's face again?"

His eyes dark with horror, Rock Casady turned and plunged downstream, stumbling, swearing in his fear and loneliness and sorrow.

At daylight, old Cat McLeod opened his eyes. For an instant, he lay still. Then he realized where he was and what he had come for, and he turned his head. Rock Casady, his gear and horse, were gone. Stumbling to his feet, McLeod slipped on his boots and walked out in his red flannels to look at the trail.

It headed south, away from Three Lakes, and away from Ben Kerr. Rock Casady was running again.

The trail south to the cañon was rough and rugged. The Appaloosa was surefooted and had a liking for the mountains, yet seemed undecided, as though the feeling persisted that he was going the wrong way. Casady stared bleakly ahead, but he saw little of the orange and red of the sandstone cliffs. He was seeing again Frank Stockman's strong, kindly face and remembering his welcome at the Three Spoke. He was remembering Sue's hand on his sleeve and her quick smile, and old Tom Bell, gnarled and worn with handling cattle and men. He drew up suddenly and turned the horse on the narrow trail. He was going back.

"Jack," he said suddenly aloud, "stick with me, boy. I'm sure going to need you now!"

Sandy Kane, grim-lipped and white of face, dismounted behind the store. Beside him was Sue Landon.

"Miss Sue," he said, "you get that buyin' done fast. Don't let none of that Vorys crowd see you. They've sure taken this town over since they shot the boss."

"All right, Sandy." She looked at him bravely and then squeezed the older man's hand. "We'll make it, all right." Her blue eyes darkened. "I wish I'd been a man, Sandy. Then the boys would come in and clean up this outfit."

"Miss Sue," he said gently, "don't fret none. Our boys are just honest cowhands. We don't have a gunfighter in the lot, nobody who could stand up to Kerr or Vorys. No man minds a scrap, but it would be plain suicide."

The girl started to enter the store, but then caught the cowhand's hand.

"Sandy," she said faintly, "look."

A tall man with broad shoulders had swung down before the store. He tied his horse with a slipknot and hitched his guns into place. Rock Casady, his hard young face bleak and desperate, stared carefully along the street.

It was only three blocks long, this street. It was dusty and warm with the noonday sun. The gray-fronted buildings looked upon the dusty canal that separated them, and a few saddled horses stamped lazily, flicking their tails at casual flies. It was like that other street, so long ago.

Casady pulled the flat brim of his black hat a little lower over his eyes. Inside, he felt sick and faint. His mouth was dry. His tongue trembled when it touched his lips. Up the street a man saw him and got slowly to his feet, staring as if hypnotized. The man backed away, and then dove into the Hackamore Saloon.

Rock Casady took a deep breath, drew his shoulders back, and started slowly down the walk. He seemed in a trance where only the sun was warm and the air was still. Voices murmured. He heard a gasp of astonishment, for these people remembered that he had whipped Pete Vorys, and they knew what he had come for.

He wore two guns now, having dug the other gun and belt from his saddlebags to join the one he had only worn in the mountains. A door slammed somewhere.

Ben Kerr stared at the face of the man in the door of the saloon.

"Ben, here comes that yellow-backed Casady! And he's wearin' a gun!"

"He is, is he?" Kerr tossed off his drink. "Fill that up, Jim! I'll be right back. This will only take a minute!"

He stepped out into the street. "Come to get it this time?" he shouted tauntingly. "Or are you runnin' again?"

Rock Casady made no reply. His footsteps echoed hollowly on the boardwalk, and he strode slowly, finishing his walk at the intersecting alley, stepping into the dust and then up on the walk again.

Ben Kerr's eyes narrowed slightly. Some sixth sense warned him that the man who faced him had subtly changed. He lifted his head a little and stared. Then he shrugged off the feeling and stepped out from the building.

"All right, yella belly! If you want it!" His hand swept down in a flashing arc and his gun came up.

Rock Casady stared down the street at the face of Ben Kerr, and it was only the face of Kerr. In his ear was Jack's voice: *Go ahead, kid! Have at it!*

Kerr's gun roared and he felt the hot breath of it bite at his face. And then suddenly, Rock Casady laughed. Within him all was light and easy, and it was almost carelessly that he stepped forward. Suddenly the .44 began to roar and buck in his hand, leaping like a live thing within his grasp. Kerr's gun flew high in the air, his knees buckled, and he fell forward on his face in the dust.

Rock Casady turned quickly toward the Hackamore. Pete Vorys stood in the door, shocked to stillness.

"All right, Pete! Do you want it or are you leavin' town?"

Vorys stared from Kerr's riddled body to the man holding the gun.

"Why, I'm leavin' town," Vorys said. "That's my roan, right there. I'll just . . ." As though stunned, he started to mount, and Rock's voice arrested him.

"No, Pete. You walk. You hoof it. And start now!" The bully of Three Lakes wet his lips and stared. Then his eyes shifted to the body in the street.

"Sure, Rock," he said, taking a step back. "I'll hoof it." Turning, stumbling a little, he started to walk. As he moved, his walk grew swifter and swifter as though something followed in his tracks.

Rock turned and looked up, and Sue Landon was standing on the boardwalk.

"Oh, Rock, you came back."

"Don't reckon I ever really left, Sue," he said slowly. "My heart's been right here all the time."

She caught his arm, and the smile in her eyes and on her lips was bright. He looked down at her.

Then he said aloud. "Thanks, Jack."

She looked up quickly. "What did you say?"

He grinned at her. "Sue," he said, "did I ever tell you about my brother? He was one grand *hombre*. Someday, I'll tell you." They walked back toward the horses, her hand on his arm.

A Strong Land Growing

At 8.00a.m. Marshal Fitz Moore left his house and walked one block west to Gard's Saloon. It was already open, and Fitz could hear Gard's swamper sweeping up the débris from the previous night.

Crossing the street, the marshal paused at the edge of the boardwalk to rub out his cigar on top of the hitching rail. As he did, he turned his eyes but not his head, glancing swiftly up the narrow street alongside the saloon. The gray horse was gone.

Fitz Moore hesitated, considering this, estimating time and probabilities. Only then did he turn and enter the Eating House just ahead of him.

The Fred Henry gang of outlaws had been operating in this corner of the territory for more than two years, but this town of Sentinel had so far escaped their attentions. Fitz Moore, who had been marshal of Sentinel for more than half of that time, had taken particular care to study the methods of the Henry outfit. He had wanted to be ready for them — and now there was also a matter of self-protection. In several of the recent raids the town marshal had been slain, and in the last three the slaying had occurred within seconds after the raid had begun.

A persistent pattern of operation had been established, and invariably the timing of the raids had coincided with the availability of large sums of money. And such a time in Sentinel, Fitz Moore knew, was now. So, unless all his reasoning was at fault, the town was marked for a raid within two hours. And he was marked for death.

The marshal was a tall, spare man with a dark, narrow face and a carefully trimmed mustache. Normally his expression was placid, only his eyes seeming alive and aware.

As he entered the restaurant now, he removed his flat-crowned black hat. His frock coat was unbuttoned, offering easy access to his Smith & Wesson .44 Russian. It was belted high and firmly on his left side just in front of his hip, butt to the right, the holster at a slight angle.

Three men and two women sat at the long community table in the Eating House, but only one of them murmured a greeting. Jack Thomas glanced up and said — "Morning, Marshal." — his voice low and friendly.

Acknowledging the greeting, the marshal sat down at the far end of the table and accepted the cup of coffee brought from the kitchen by the Chinese cook.

With his mind closed to the drift of conversation from the far end of the table, he considered the situation that faced him. His days began in the same identical manner, with a survey of the town from each of the six windows of his house. This morning he had seen a gray horse tied behind Peterson's unused corral, where it would not be seen by a casual glance.

With field glasses the marshal had examined the horse. It was streaked with the salt of dried sweat, evidence of hard riding. There were still some dark, damp spots, implying that the horse had been ridden not long before, and the fact that it was still bridled and saddled indicated that it would soon be ridden again. The brand was a Rocking R, not a local iron.

When Fitz Moore had returned to his living room, he had seated himself and opened his Plutarch. For an hour he read quietly and with genuine pleasure, finally rising to glance from the back window. The gray horse had not been moved.

At 8.00, when he had left for breakfast, the horse was still there, but by the time he had walked a block, it was gone. And there lingered in the air a faint dust.

Down the arroyo, of course, in the access to cañons, forest, and mountains, there was concealment and water. Taking into consideration the cool night, the sweat-marked horse — not less than six miles to the point of rendezvous. The rider of the gray obviously had been making some final check with a local source of information. To get back to the rendezvous, discuss the situation and return, he had two hours, perhaps a little more. He would deal in minimums.

The marshal lighted a cigar, accepted a fresh cup of coffee from the Chinese cook, and leaned back in his chair. He was a man of simple tastes and many appreciations. He knew little of cattle and less of mining, but two things he did know. He knew guns and he knew men.

He was aware of the cool gray eyes of the young woman, the only person present who he did not know. There was about her a nagging familiarity that disturbed him. He tasted his coffee and glanced out the window. Reason warned him that he should be suspicious of any stranger in town at this time, yet instinct told him this girl warranted no suspicion.

The Emporium Bank would be open in approximately an hour. A few minutes later Barney Gard would leave his saloon and cross the street with the Saturday and Sunday receipts. It would be a considerable sum.

The Emporium safe would be unlocked by that time, and, since they had been accepting money from ranchers and dust from miners, there would be plenty of ready cash there. In one hour there would be $20,000 in negotiable cash within easy reach of grasping fingers and ready guns. And the Henry gang had taken steps that had made them aware of this. The marshal realized this now.

He did not know the name of the stranger who had played poker with the Catfish Kid last week. He had known the face. It had been that of a man who had been in Tascosa with the bandit leader, Fred Henry, two years ago. Tied to this was the fact that the Rocking R brand was registered to one Harvey Danuser, alias Dick Mawson, the fastest gun hand in the Henry outfit.

He was suddenly aware that a question had been addressed to him. "What would you do, Marshal," Jack Thomas was saying, "if the Henry gang raided Sentinel?"

42

Fitz Moore glanced at the burning end of his cigar. Then he looked up, his eyes level and appraising. "I think," he said mildly, "I should have to take steps."

The marshal was not a precipitate man. Reputed to be fast with a gun, that speed had yet to be proved locally. Once a few years ago, he had killed the wrong man. He hoped never to make that mistake again.

So far he had enforced the peace in Sentinel by shrewd judgment of character, appreciation of developing situations, and tactical moves that invariably left him in command. Authorized to employ an assistant, he had not done so. He preferred to work alone, as he lived alone. He was, he acknowledged — but only to himself — a lonely man. If he possessed any capacity for affection or friendship, it had not been obvious to the people of Sentinel. Yet this was an added strength. No one presumed to take him lightly or to expect favoritism.

Long ago he had been considered a brilliant conversationalist, and even in a time when a cowhand's saddlebags might carry a volume of Shakespeare as often as one by Ned Buntline, he was a widely read man. He had been a captain in the cavalry of the United States, a colonel in a Mexican revolution, a shotgun messenger for Wells, Fargo, and a division superintendent on the Butterfield Stage Line.

Naturally he knew considerable about the Henry gang. The outlaws had been operating for several years, but only of late had exhibited a tendency to shoot first and talk later. This seemed to indicate that at least one of the gang had become a ruthless killer.

All three of the marshals who had recently been killed had been shot in the back. It indicated that a *modus operandi* had been established. First kill the marshal, then rob the town. With the marshal dead, resistance was unlikely before the bandits could make their escape.

Fitz Moore dusted the ash from his cigar. He thought that gray horse had been standing long enough for the sweat to dry, which meant he had been ridden into town before daybreak. At that hour everything was closed, and he saw no one on the street, which indicated that the rider went inside somewhere. And that indicated he not only knew where to go at that hour but was sure he would be welcomed.

The Henry gang had an accomplice in Sentinel. When the rider of the gray horse had left town, that accomplice undoubtedly had been awake, and with a raid imminent it was unlikely he would go back to sleep. What place more likely for him to be than in this café? Here he could see who was around and have a chance to judge the marshal's temper.

Had anyone entered just before he had arrived? Fitz Moore knew everyone in the room except the girl with the gray eyes. She was watching him now.

Each of the others had a reason to be here at this hour. Barney Gard had opened his saloon and left it to the ministrations of the swamper. Jack Thomas directed the destinies of the livery stable. Johnny Haven, when he wasn't getting drunk and trying to tree the town, was a hardworking young cowhand and thoroughly reliable.

44

The older of the two women present was Mary Jameson, a plump and gossipy widow, the town's milliner, dressmaker, and Niagara of conversation. When she finished her breakfast, she would walk three doors down the street and open her shop.

But the girl with the gray eyes? Her face was both delicate and strong, her hair dark and lovely, and she had a certain air of being to the manor born. Perhaps it was because she did possess that air, like someone from the marshal's own past, that she seemed familiar. And because she was the sort of girl . . . But it was too late for that now. He was being a fool.

Yet there was a definite antagonism in her eyes when she looked at him, and he could not account for it. He was accustomed to the attention of women — something he had always had — but not antagonistic attention.

Disturbed by this and by that haunting familiarity, as of a forgotten name that hangs upon the lips yet will not be spoken, he shook off these questions to consider his more immediate problem.

The marshal glanced thoughtfully at Johnny Haven. The young cowboy was staring sourly at his plate, devoting his attention almost exclusively to his coffee. Over his right temple was a swelling and a cut, and this, coupled with his hangover, had left Johnny in a disgruntled mood. Last night had seen the end of his monthly spree, and the cut was evidence of the marshal's attention.

Johnny caught the marshal's glance and scowled irritably. "You sure leave a man with a headache, Marshal. Did you have to slug me with that gun?"

Fitz Moore once more dusted the ash from his cigar. "I didn't have an axe handle, and nothing else seemed suitable for the job." He added casually: "Of course, I might have shot you."

Johnny Haven was aware of this. He knew perfectly well that most marshals would have done just that, but coming from Fitz Moore it was almost an explanation.

"Is it so easy to kill men?" It was the girl with the gray eyes who spoke, in a voice that was low and modulated, but also in it contempt was plain.

"That depends," Fitz Moore replied quietly, "on the man doing the shooting and upon the circumstances."

"I think" — her eyes seemed to blaze momentarily — "that you would find it easy to kill. You might even enjoy killing. That is, if you were able to feel anything at all."

The depth of emotion in her voice was so apparent that even Johnny turned to look at her. She was dead white, her eyes large.

The marshal's expression did not change. He knew that Johnny Haven understood, as any Westerner would. Johnny himself had given cause for shooting on more than one occasion. He also knew that what Marshal Moore had just said was more of an explanation than he had ever given to any other man. Fitz Moore had arrested Johnny Haven six times in as many months, for after every payday Johnny came to town hunting trouble.

The girl's tone and words had in them an animosity for which none of them could account, and it left them uneasy.

Barney Gard got to his feet and dropped a dollar on the table. Johnny Haven followed him out, and then the milliner left. Jack Thomas loitered over his coffee.

"That Henry bunch has got me worried, Marshal," he said. "Want me to get down the old scatter-gun, just in case?"

Fitz Moore watched Barney Gard through the window. The saloon man had paused on the walk to talk to Johnny Haven. Under the stubble of beard, Johnny's face looked clean and strong, reminding the marshal again, as it had before, of the face of another boy, scarcely older.

"It won't be necessary," Moore replied. "I'll handle them in my own way, in my own time. It's my job, you know."

"Isn't that a bit foolish? To refuse help?"

The contempt still in the girl's voice stirred him, but his expression revealed nothing. He nodded gravely.

"Why, I suppose it might be, ma'am, but it's the job they hired me to do."

"Figured I'd offer," Thomas said, unwilling to let the matter drop. "You tell me what you figure to do, and I'll be glad to help."

"Another time." The marshal tasted his coffee again and looked directly at the girl. "You are new in Sentinel. Will you be staying long?"

"Not long."

"You have relatives here?"

"No."

He waited, but no explanation was offered. Fitz Moore was puzzled, and he studied her out of the corners of his eyes. There was no sound but the ticking of the big old-fashioned clock on the shelf.

The girl sat very still, the delicate line of her profile bringing to him a faint, lost feeling, a nostalgia from his boyhood when there was perfume in the air, bluegrass, picket fences . . . And then he remembered!

Thomas got to his feet. He was a big, swarthy man, always untidy, a bulge of fat pushing his wide belt. "You need my help, Marshal," he said, "you call on me."

Fitz Moore permitted himself one of his rare smiles. "If there is trouble, Jack," he said, as he glanced up, "you'll be among the first to know."

The clock ticked off the slow seconds after the door closed, and then the marshal spoke into the silence.

"Why have you come here? What can you do in this place?"

She looked down at her hands. "All I have is here . . . a little farther west. I left the stage only to hire a rig . . . And then I heard your name, and I wanted to see what manner of man it would be who could kill his best friend."

He got to his feet. At this moment he knew better than ever before what loneliness meant.

"You must not judge too quickly," he said quietly. "Each man deserves to be judged against the canvas of his time and his country."

"There is only one way to judge a killer."

"Wait. You will know what I mean if you will wait a little while. And stay off the street today." He walked to the door and stopped with his hand upon the latch. "He used to tell me about you. We talked of you, and I came to feel that I knew you well. I had hoped . . . before it happened . . . that we could meet. But in a different way than this. What will happen today I want you to see. I do not believe you lack the courage to watch what happens, nor to revise your opinions if you feel you have been mistaken. Your brother, as you were advised in my letter, was killed by accident."

"But you shot him. You were in a great hurry to kill."

"He ran up behind me."

"To help you."

"I had seen him a hundred miles from there. It was . . . quick. At such a time one does not think. One acts."

"Kill first," she said bitterly, "and look afterward."

His face was stiff. "I am afraid that is just what one does. I am sorry, Julia."

He lifted the latch. "When you see what is done today, try to think how else it might have been handled. If you cannot see this as I do, then before night comes you will think me more cruel than you have before. But if you understand, where there is understanding there is no hate."

Outside the door he paused and surveyed the street with care. Not much longer now.

Across from him was Gard's Saloon. One block down the street, his own office and his home, and across from it, just a little beyond, an abandoned barn.

49

He studied it thoughtfully and then glanced again at Gard's and at the bank, diagonally across, beyond the milliner's shop.

It would happen here, upon this dusty street, between these buildings. Here men would die, and it was his mission to be sure the right man lived and the bad died. He was expendable, but which was he? Good or bad?

Fitz Moore knew every alley, every door, every corner in this cluster of heat-baked, alkali-stamped buildings that soon would be an arena for life and death. His eyes turned thoughtfully again to the abandoned barn. It projected several feet beyond the otherwise carefully lined buildings. The big door through which hay had once been loaded gaped widely. So little time!

He knew what they said about him. "Ain't got a friend in town," he had overheard Mrs. Jameson say. "Stays to hisself in that long old house. Got it full of books, folks say. But kill you quick as a wink, he would. He's cold . . . mighty cold."

But was he? Was he? When he had first come to this town, he found it a shambles, wrecked by a passing trail-herd crew. He had found it terrorized by two dozen gunmen and looted by card sharks and thieves. Robbery had been the order of the day, and murder all too frequent. It had been six months now since there had been a robbery of any kind, and more than nine months since the last killing. Did that count for nothing at all?

He took out a cigar and bit off the end. What was the matter with him today? He had not felt like this in years. Was it, as they say happens to a drowning man, that his life was passing before his eyes just before the end? Or was it seeing Julia Heath, the sum total of all he had ever wanted in a girl? And, realizing who she was, knew how impossible all he had ever longed for had become?

They had talked of it, he and Tom Heath, and he knew Tom had written to Julia, suggesting she come West because he had found the man for her. And two weeks later Tom had been dead with Fitz Moore's bullet in his heart.

The marshal walked on along the street of false-fronted, weather-beaten buildings. Squalid and dismal as they looked, crouching here where desert and mountains met, the town was changing. It was growing with the hopes of the people, with their changing needs. This spring, for the first time, flowers had been planted in the yard of the house beyond the church, and in front of another house a tree had been trimmed.

From being a haphazard collection of buildings, catering to the transient needs of a transient people, the town of Sentinel was becoming vital, acquiring a consciousness of the future, a sense of belonging. A strong land growing, a land that would give birth to strong sons who could build and plant and harvest.

Fitz Moore turned into the empty alley between the Emporium and the abandoned barn, which was a relic of over-ambition during a boom. And thoughts persisted. With the marshal dead, and the town helpless . . .

But how had the outlaw gang planned to kill him? For that it had been planned was to him a certainty. And it must be done and done quickly when the time came.

The loft of the barn commanded a view of the street. The outlaws would come into town riding toward the barn, and somewhere along that street, easily covered by a rifleman concealed in the barn, the marshal of Sentinel would be walking.

He climbed the stairs to the loft. The dust on the steps had been disturbed. At the top a board creaked under his feet, and a rat scurried away. The loft was wide and empty. Only dust and wisps of hay.

From that wide door the raid might be stopped, but this was not the place for him. His place was down there in that hot, dusty street, where his presence might count. There was much to do. And now there was only a little time.

Returning to his quarters, Fitz Moore thrust an extra gun into his pocket and belted on a third. Then he put two shotguns into his wood sack. Nobody would be surprised to see him with the sack, for he always carried firewood in it that he got from the pile in back of Gard's.

He saw Jack Thomas, sitting in a chair before the livery stable. Barney Gard came from the saloon, glanced at the marshal, and then went back inside. Fitz Moore paused, relighting his dead cigar.

The topic of what would happen here if the Henry gang attempted a raid was not a new one. He had heard much speculation. Some men, like Thomas, had brought it up before, trying to feel him out, to discover what he thought, what he would do.

Jack Thomas turned his big head on his thick neck and glanced toward the marshal. He was a good-natured man, but too inquisitive, too dirty.

Johnny Haven, sitting on the steps of the saloon porch, looked at the marshal and grinned. He was a powerful, aggressive young man.

"How's the town clown?" he asked.

Moore paused, drawing deep on his cigar, permitting himself a glance toward the loft door, almost sixty yards away and across the street. Deliberately he had placed himself in line with the best shooting position.

"Johnny," he said, "if anything happens to me, I want you to have this job. If nothing does happen to me, I want you for my deputy."

Young Haven could not have been more astonished, but he also was deeply moved. He looked up as if he believed the marshal had been suddenly touched by the heat. Aside from the words, the very fact that Marshal Moore had ventured a personal remark was astonishing.

"You're twenty-six, Johnny, and it's time you grew up. You've played at being a bad man long enough. I've looked the town over, and you're the man I want."

Johnny — Tom. He avoided thinking of them together, yet there was a connection. Tom once had been a good man, too, but now he was a good man gone. Johnny was a good man, much like Tom, although walking the hairline of the law.

Johnny Haven was profoundly impressed. To say that he admired and respected this tall, composed man was no more than the truth. After his first forcible arrest by Fitz Moore, Johnny had been furious enough to beat him up or kill him, but each time he had come to town he had found himself neatly boxed and helpless.

Nor had Fitz Moore ever taken unfair advantage, never striking one blow more than essential and never keeping the young cowhand in jail one hour longer than necessary. And Johnny Haven was honest enough to realize that he never could have handled the situation as well.

Anger had resolved into reluctant admiration. Only his native stubbornness and the pride of youth had prevented him from giving up the struggle. "Why pick on me?" He spoke roughly to cover his emotion. "You won't be quitting."

There was a faint suggestion of movement from the loft. The marshal glanced at his watch. 10.02.

"Johnny" — the sudden change of tone brought Johnny's head up sharply — "when the shooting starts, there are two shotguns in this sack. Get behind the end of the water trough and use one of them. Shoot from under the trough. It's safer."

Two riders walked their mounts into the upper end of the street, almost a half block away. Two men on

54

powerful horses, better horses than would be found on any cow ranch.

Three more riders came from a space between the buildings, from the direction of Peterson's Corral. One of them was riding a gray horse. They were within twenty yards when Barney Gard came from the saloon, carrying two canvas bags. He was headed for the bank when one of the horsemen swung his mount to a route that would cut across Barney's path.

"Shotgun in the sack, Gard." The marshal's voice was conversational.

Then, as sunlight glinted on a rifle barrel in the loft door, Fitz Moore took one step forward, drawing as he moved, and the thunder of the rifle merged with the bark of his own gun. Then the rifle clattered, falling, and an arm lay loosely in the loft door.

The marshal had turned instantly. "All right, Henry!" His voice rang like a trumpet call in the narrow street. "You're asking for it! Take it!"

There was no request for surrender. The rope awaited these men, and death rode their guns and hands.

As one man they drew, and the marshal sprang into the street, landing flat-footed and firing. The instant of surprise had been his. And his first shot, only a dancing second after the bullet that had killed the man in the loft, struck Fred Henry over the belt buckle.

Behind and to the marshal's right a shotgun's deep roar blasted the sunlit morning. The man on the gray horse died falling, his gun throwing a useless shot into the hot, still air.

Horses reared, and a cloud of dust and gunpowder arose, stabbed through with crimson flame and the hoarse bark of guns.

A rider leaped his horse at the marshal, but Fitz Moore stood his ground and fired. The rider's face seemed to disintegrate under the impact of the bullet.

And then there was silence. The roaring was gone and only the faint smells lingered — the acrid tang of gunpowder, of blood in the dust, of the brighter crimson scent of blood on a saddle.

Johnny Haven got up slowly from behind the horse trough. Barney Gard stared around as if he had just awakened, his hands gripping a shotgun.

There was a babble of sound then, of people running into the street. And a girl with gray eyes was watching. Those eyes seemed to reach across the street and into the heart of the marshal.

"Only one shot!" Barney Gard exclaimed. "I got off only one shot and missed that one!"

"The Henry gang wiped out!" yelled an excited citizen. "Wait'll Thomas hears of this!"

"He won't be listenin," somebody else said. "They got him."

Fitz Moore turned like a duelist. "I got him," he said flatly. "He was their man. Tried all morning to find out what I'd do if they showed up . . ."

An hour later Johnny Haven followed the marshal into the street. Four men were dead and two were in jail. "How did you know, Marshal?"

56

"You learn, Johnny. You learn or you die. That's your lesson for today. Learn to be in the right place at the right time and keep your own counsel. You'll be getting my job." His cigar was gone. He bit the end from a fresh one and went on. "Jack Thomas was the only man the rider of the gray horse I told you I saw could have reached without crossing the street. He wouldn't have left the horse he'd need for a quick getaway on the wrong side of the street. Besides, I'd been doubtful of Thomas. He was prying too much."

When he entered the Eating House, Julia Heath was at the table again. She was white and shaken. He spoke to her.

"I'm sorry, Julia, but now you see how little time there is for a man when guns are drawn. These men would have taken the money honest men worked to get, and they would have killed as they have killed before. Such men know only the law of the gun." He placed his hands on the table. "I should have known you at once, but I never thought . . . after what happened . . . that you would come, even to settle the estate. He was proud of you, Julia, and he was my best friend."

"But you killed him."

Marshal Moore gestured toward the street. "It was like that. Guns exploding, a man dying under my gun, and then running feet behind me in a town where I had no friends. I thought Tom was on his ranch in Colorado. I killed the man who was firing at me, turned, and fired toward the running feet. And killed my friend, your brother."

She knew then how it must have been for this man, and she was silent.

"And now?" she murmured.

"My job will go to Johnny Haven, but I'm going to stay here and help this town grow, help it become a community of homes, use some of the things I know that have nothing to do with guns. This" — he gestured toward the street — "should end it for a while. In the breathing space we can mature, settle down, change the houses into homes, and bring some beauty into this makeshift."

She was silent again, looking down at the table. At last she spoke, her voice barely audible. "It . . . it's worth doing."

"It will be." He looked at his unlighted cigar. "You'll be going to settle Tom's property. When you come back, if you want to, you might stop off again. If you do, I'll be waiting to see you."

She looked at him, seeing beyond the coldness, seeing the man her brother must have known. "I think I shall. I think I'll stop . . . when I come back."

Out in the street a man was raking dust over the blood. Back of the old barn a hen cackled, and somewhere a pump started to complain rustily, drawing clear water from a deep, cold well.

Lit a Shuck for Texas

The Sandy Kid slid the roan down the steep bank into the draw and fast-walked it over to where Jasper Wald sat his big iron-gray stallion. The Kid, who was nineteen and new to this range, pulled up a short distance from his boss. That gray stallion was mighty near as mean as Wald himself.

"Howdy, boss! Look what I found back over in that rough country east of here."

Wald scowled at the rock the rider held out. "I ain't payin' you to hunt rocks," he declared. "You get back there in the breaks roundin' up strays like I'm payin' you for."

"I figgered you'd be interested. I reckon this here's gold."

"Gold?" Wald's laugh was sardonic, and he threw a contemptuous glance at the cowhand. "In this country? You're a fool!"

The Sandy Kid shoved the rock back in his chaps pocket and swung his horse back toward the brush, considerably deflated. Maybe it was silly to think of finding gold here, but that rock sure enough looked it, and it was heavy. He reckoned he'd heard somewhere that gold was a mighty heavy metal.

When he was almost at the edge of the badlands, he saw a steer heading toward the thick brush, so he gave the roan a taste of the diggers and spiked his horse's tail after the steer. That old ladino could run like a deer, and it headed out for those high rocks like a tramp after a chuck wagon, but when it neared the rocks, the mossyhorn ducked and, head down, cut off at right angles, racing for the willows.

Beyond the willows was a thicket of brush, rock, and cactus that made riding precarious and roping almost suicidal, and once that steer got into the tangle beyond, he was gone. The Kid shook out a loop and hightailed it after the steer, but it was a shade far for good roping when he made his cast. Even at that, he'd have made it, but just as his rope snagged the steer, the roan's hoof went into a gopher hole, and the Sandy Kid sailed right off over the roan's ears.

As he hit the ground all in a lump, he caught a glimpse of the ladino. Wheeling around, head down with about four or five feet of horn, it started for him.

With a yelp, the Kid grabbed for his gun, but it was gone, so he made a frantic leap for a cleft in the ground. Even as he rolled into it, he felt the hot breath of the steer, or thought he did.

The steer went over the cleft, scuffling dust down on the cowboy. When the Kid looked around, he saw he was lying in a crack that was about three feet wide and at least thirty feet deep. He had landed on a ledge that all but closed off the crack for several feet.

Warily he eased his head over the edge and then jerked back with a gasp, for the steer was standing, red-eyed and mean, not over ten feet away and staring right at him.

Digging out the makings, the Kid rolled a cigarette. After all, why get cut up about it? The steer would go away after a while, and then it would be safe to come out. In the meantime it was mighty cool here and pleasant enough, what with the sound of falling water and all.

The thought of water reminded the Kid that he was thirsty. He studied the situation and decided that with care he could climb to the bottom without any danger. Once down where the water was, he could get a drink. He was not worried, for, when he had looked about, he had seen his horse, bridle reins trailing, standing not far away. The roan would stand forever that way.

His six-gun, which had been thrown from his holster when he fell, also lay up there on the grass. It was not over twenty feet from the rim of the crevice, and, once it was in his hand, it would be a simple thing to knock off that steer. Getting the pistol was quite another thing. With that steer on the prod, it would be suicide to try.

When he reached the bottom of the crevice, he peered around in the vague light. At noon, or close to that, it would be bright down here, but at any other time it would be thick with shadows. Kneeling by the thin trickle of water, the Kid drank his fill. Lifting his face from the water, he looked downstream and almost jumped out of his skin when he saw a grinning skull.

The Sandy Kid was no pilgrim. He had fought Apaches and Comanches, and twice he had been over the trail to Dodge. But seeing a skull grinning at him from a distance of only a few feet did nothing to make him feel comfortable and at ease.

"By grab, looks like I ain't the first to tumble into this place," he said. "That *hombre* must have broken a leg and starved to death."

Yet when he walked over and examined the skeleton, he could see he was wrong. The man had been shot through the head.

Gingerly the Kid moved the skull. There was a hole on the other side, too, and a bullet flattened against the rock. He was astonished.

"Well, now, somebody shot this *hombre* while he laid here," the Kid decided.

Squatting on his haunches, the Sandy Kid puffed his cigarette and studied the situation. Long experience in reading sign had made it easy for his eyes to see what should be seen. A few things he noticed now. This man, already wounded, had fallen or been pushed into the crack, and then a man with a gun had leaned over the edge above and shot him through the head.

There was a notch in his belt that must have been cut by a bullet, and one knee had been broken by a bullet, for the slug was still there, embedded in the joint. The Kid was guessing about the notch, but from the look of things and the way the man was doubled up, it looked like he had been hurt pretty bad aside from the knee. The shirt was gone except for a few shreds, and among the rocky débris there were a few buttons, an old pocket knife, and some coins. The boots, dried and stiff, were not a horseman's boots, but the high-topped, flat-heeled type that miners wear. A rusted six-shooter lay a bit farther downstream, and the Kid retrieved it. After a few minutes he determined that the gun was still fully loaded.

"Probably never got a shot at the skunk," the Sandy Kid said thoughtfully. "Well, now, ain't this a pretty mess?"

When he studied the skeleton further, he noticed something under the ribs that he had passed over, thinking it a rock. Now he saw it was a small leather sack that the dead man had evidently carried inside his shirt. The leather was dry and stiff, and it ripped when he tried to open it. Within were several fragments of the same ore the Kid had himself found.

Tucking the samples and the remnants of the sack under a rocky ledge, the Kid stuck the rusty six-shooter in his belt and climbed back to the ledge, where a cautious look showed that the ladino was gone.

The roan pricked up its ears and whinnied, not at all astonished that this peculiar master of his should come crawling out of the ground. The Kid had lost his rope, which was probably still trailing from the steer's horns, but he was not thinking of that. He was thinking of the murdered man.

When he awakened the next morning, he rolled over on his side and stared around the bunkhouse. Everyone was still asleep, and then he realized that it was Sunday.

Wald was nowhere around when the Kid headed for the cook shack. Smoke was rising slowly, for Cholly Cooper, the best cook on that range, was conscientious. When you wanted breakfast, you got it, early or late.

The Sandy Kid was glad that Wald was not around, for he had no love for his morose, quick-to-anger boss.

It was not a pleasant outfit to ride for, Cooper being the only friendly one in the bunch. Jasper Wald never spoke, except to give an order or to criticize in a dry, sarcastic voice. He was about forty, tough and hard-bitten. Rumor had it that he had killed more than one man. His two permanent hands were Jack Swarr, a burly Kansas man, always unshaven, and Dutch Schweitzer, a lean German who drank heavily.

"Hi, Sandy." Cholly waved a fork at him. "Set yourself down and I'll get some coffee. Up early, ain't you?"

"Uhn-huh." The Kid pulled the thick cup toward him. "Sort of reckoned I'd ride up to the Forks. Few things I need. Shirts and stuff."

Cholly dished out a couple of thick slabs of beef and four eggs. "Better eat," he said. "I wouldn't want you puttin' on them shirts on an empty stomach." While Cholly refilled the Kid's cup, he said in a low voice: "What did you all do to the boss? He was shore riled up when he came in and saw you hadn't showed up with the rest of the hands."

"Reckon he was just sore. I tied in with an old mossyhorn up in the breaks and lost my rope. Durned steer had one horn, looked long enough for two steers, and a stub on the other end."

Cooper chuckled. "You ain't the first who lost a rope on Ol' Stob. You were lucky not to get killed."

"Rough country, over thataway," the Sandy Kid suggested. "Ever been over there?"

"No farther'n the creek, and I don't aim to. Only one man ever knowed that country, unless it was the Apaches, and that was Jim Kurland. He always claimed there was gold over there, but most folks just laughed at him."

"Rancher?"

"No, sort of a prospector. He mined some, I guess, afore he came here. Dead now, I reckon. He headed off into that country about a year ago and nobody ever saw hide nor hair of him again. His wife, she died about three, four months ago, and his daughter works down to Wright's Store. She handles the post office in there, mostly."

Jim Kurland. It was a name to remember. The Sandy Kid knew he was walking on dangerous ground. The killer of Kurland, if it was his skeleton the Kid had found, was probably still around, and any mention of Kurland's name might lead to trouble. It would be wise to proceed with caution.

The Sandy Kid was no hero. He had never toted a badge, and like most cowhands of his day he looked upon the law as a nuisance originated mainly to keep riders from having a good time. He went his own way, and, if someone made trouble for him, he figured to handle it himself. He would be ashamed to ask for help and figured all sheriffs were the same.

He was interested in gold. If there was a mine as rich as that ore seemed to indicate, he wanted it. Why, with a little gold a man could buy a spread of his own and stock it with those new whiteface cattle that carried so much more beef than a longhorn. A man could do right well with a little money to go on.

When he rode into the Forks, he headed right for the store. He was not planning on doing any drinking this day. It was Sunday, but Sim Wright kept his store open seven days a week the year around. The Sandy Kid, who was a lean six feet and with a shock of sandy hair and mild gray eyes, swung down from the roan and crossed the boardwalk to the store.

At first he thought it was empty. Then he saw the girl who stood behind the counter, her eyes on him.

He jerked his hat from his head and went toward her. "Ma'am," he said, "I better get me a couple of shirts. You got anything with checks in it?"

"Big checks?" She smiled at him.

"Uhn-huh, that's right."

She shoved him the shirts, one of them with black and white checks as big as those on a checkerboard.

He fingered them thoughtfully. Then he said: "Ma'am, is your name Kurland?"

"That's my last name. My first name is Betty."

"Mine's Sandy," he told her. "They call me the Sandy Kid."

He hesitated, and then slid a hand into his pocket and took out the pocket knife and laid it on the shirts.

Her face went white as she caught it up. She looked at the Kid. "Where did you get this?"

Slowly, carefully he told her. As he talked, she stared at him with wide eyes. "You think," she asked when he had finished, "that he was murdered? But why?"

68

"He had gold samples, ma'am. Folks will do a powerful lot for gold. I would myself. I sort of figured I'd keep quiet about this, and sort of hunt that claim myself, and, when I found it, I'd stake her out. Then I heard about you, an' I figgered you'd like to know about your pappy and have him buried proper."

"Who killed him?"

"That I don't know. I reckon, if a body was to try, he could find out, but you'd have to keep still about findin' him for a while."

"If I keep still, will you find the murderer? If you do, I'll give you that claim."

"No, ma'am, I couldn't take your claim. Menfolk in my family wasn't raised no such way. But I don't have a particle of use for a coyote that would murder a man like that, so, if you want, I'll have a look around in my spare time."

Her eyes were large and dark. It was nice looking into them. The Sandy Kid reckoned he had never looked into eyes that were like hers. And her lips — she had right nice lips. Not too full and not thin, either. He liked that. Her neck was sure white. She was smiling at him, amused.

He flushed a deep red. "Reckon you must think I never saw a girl before," he said. "Well, I reckon mebbe I never did really look at one. Somehow, they never sort of called themselves to mind."

"Thank you, Sandy."

All the way back to the ranch he was thinking how nice that name sounded from her lips.

The Bar W lay like an ugly sore in the bottom of the flat. There were three adjoining pole corrals, an unpainted frame bunkhouse, and a ranch house of adobe. The cook shack was also adobe, and there was smoke coming from the chimney when he rode in with his shirts.

It was still quite early, for the ranch was only a short piece from town. He unsaddled the roan and walked back toward the cook shack for coffee. They were all there. Nobody said anything when he came in, but Cholly threw him a warning glance. The Kid got a cup and filled it with coffee. Then he sat down.

"What happened to you last night?" Wald demanded, glaring at him across the table.

"Me? I had me a run-in with that Old Stob horned ladino. Lost my rope."

"You still got that rock?"

"That?" The Sandy Kid shrugged carelessly. "No. I threw it away. Reckon it was just iron pyrites or something."

Nothing more was said, but he felt uncomfortable. He had found Jasper Wald an unpleasant man to work for, and the sooner he got himself another job the better off he would be. There was something in Wald's baleful glance that disturbed him.

"In the mornin'," Wald said after a few minutes, "you work that Thumb Butte country."

The Kid nodded, but made no comment. The Thumb Butte area was six miles across the valley from the badlands where he'd had the run-in with Old Stob, that red-eyed mossyhorn. Was it accident or design that had caused Wald to send him to the other side of the ranch?

Yet the next day he realized that his new working ground had advantages of its own. He worked hard all morning and rounded up and turned into a mountain corral forty head of cattle that he had combed out of the piñons.

Switching his saddle to a bay pony, he took off into the draws that led south and west, away from the ranch. An hour's riding brought him to the Argo trail, and he cantered along to the little town at Argo Springs. Here was the only Land Office within two hundred miles or more where a mining claim could be registered.

A quick check of the books, offered him by an obliging justice of the peace who also served in five or six other capacities, showed him that no mining claim had been located in the vicinity of the badlands. Hence, if the killer of Jim Kurland had found the claim, he was working it on the sly. He did some further checking, but the discovery he made was by accident. It came out of a blue sky when Pete Mallinger, at the Wells, Fargo office, noticed his brand.

"Bar W, eh? You bring one of them boxes over here? The ones Wald's been shippin' to El Paso?"

"Me? No, I just rode over to get myself some smoking." He grinned confidentially. "The boss doesn't even know I'm gone."

"I wouldn't let him ketch you. He's a tough one, that Jasper Wald is. Throw a gun on a man soon's look at him. Got money, too, he has. He's buyin' up most of that Agua Dulce Cañon country."

71

The Sandy Kid rolled a smoke and listened, his eyes sweeping the narrow street with its hitching rails and clapboarded buildings. Jasper Wald was not making enough on the Bar W to buy any land, not even with all his free-and-easy branding operations. Nothing you could really complain about, but nevertheless the Bar W brand was showing up on almost everything on the range that came within sight of a Bar W hand.

Before he left, the Kid managed to get his hands on the address in El Paso. The boxes were being shipped to Henry Wald, a brother of Jasper, and they were notably heavy.

The Sandy Kid strolled thoughtfully away from the door of the Wells, Fargo office and crossed the dusty street to the saloon. He might as well have a drink while he was here. He pushed through the swinging doors into the bare, untidy barroom. Dutch Schweitzer was leaning an elbow on the bar, staring at him.

"Howdy." The Sandy Kid strolled up to the bar and ordered a drink. "Looks like we've both strayed on the same morning."

Dutch looked at him with sullen eyes. "No, I'm on the job. The boss sent me over here. He didn't send you."

"Sure he didn't. I rounded up enough stock for a full day in that country where I'm working. It's dry work, so I ambled over for a drink."

"At the Wells, Fargo office?"

The Kid shrugged. He picked up his glass and tossed off his drink. "I'm on my way back," he said, and turned to go. Schweitzer's voice halted him.

"Wait."

The Sandy Kid turned. Suddenly he felt cold. He had never met a man in a gun battle, but there was cold deadliness in the big German's eyes. The Kid stood with his feet apart a little, and his mouth felt dry. He felt sure Dutch meant to kill him.

Schweitzer had been drinking but was not drunk. The man had an enormous capacity for liquor, yet he rarely drank to the point where he was unsteady or loose talking. Only when he drank he grew mean and cruel.

"You're a smart kid. Too blamed smart," he said meaningfully.

Two men in the back of the room got up and eased out through the rear door. The Sandy Kid could see that the bartender was obviously frightened.

Curiously the Kid was not. He watched Dutch carefully, aware that the man was spoiling for trouble, that he had a fierce, driving urge for brutality. Some inner canker gnawed at him, some bitter hatred that he seemed to nurse for everything and everybody. The Sandy Kid knew it was not personal animosity. It was simply that in these moods Dutch Schweitzer was a killer, and only the tiniest spark was needed to touch him off.

In that mental clarity that comes in moments of great stress, the Kid found himself aware of many things — a wet ring on the bar where his glass had stood, the half empty bottle near Schweitzer, the two empty tables in the back of the room. He saw the sickly pallor on the bartender's flabby face and the yellow hairs on the backs of Schweitzer's hands.

"You stick your nose into trouble." Schweitzer lifted the bottle with his left hand to pour a drink. Then his face suddenly twisted with blind, bitter fury, and he jerked the bottle up to throw it at the Kid.

Afterward, the Kid could never remember any impulse or feeling. He simply drew and fired without any thought or plan, and he fired at the bottle.

It exploded in a shower of glass and drenched Schweitzer with whiskey. He sprang back, amazed, and, when he looked up at the Kid, he was cold sober. Slowly, his eyes wide and his face pale, Schweitzer lifted his hands in a gesture of surrender. "I ain't drawin'," he said, astonishment making his voice thick. "I ain't makin' a move."

"See that you don't," the Sandy Kid said flatly. He glared at the bartender, and then backed through the swinging doors and holstered his gun. With a wary eye on the saloon, he crossed to his horse, mounted, and rode out of town.

He moved in a sort of daze. He was no gunfighter and had never fancied himself as such. He was only a drifting cowhand who dreamed of someday owning his own spread. He had never found any occasion for split-second drawing, although he had practiced, of course. He had been wearing a six-gun for years, and he practiced throwing it hour after hour, but more to ease the monotony of long nights on night guard than from any desire for skill. It had been something to do, like riffling cards, playing solitaire, or juggling stones.

Like all Texas men of his time he had done his share of fighting and he had done a lot of shooting. He knew he was a good shot and that he nearly always got what he went after, but shooting as quickly and accurately as he had done in the saloon had never been considered.

Out of town, he did not ride away. When Dutch Schweitzer returned, he would tell Jasper Wald what had happened. There would be trouble then, the Kid knew, and the least he could expect would be to be fired. Yet there was something he would do before he left town. Riding around the town in the juniper-clad hills, he dismounted and seated himself for a long wait.

He saw Dutch ride out a short time later. He saw the streets become less peopled, and he saw the sun go down. When it was dark, he moved down to the Wells, Fargo office. When Dutch left, he had been driving a buckboard, and that meant something to the Kid.

Using his knife, he cut away the putty around a pane of glass, and then reached through and unfastened the window. Raising it, he crawled in.

For an instant he stood still, listening. There was no sound, so he struck a match and, shielding it in his hands, looked around for the box. He identified it quickly enough by the address. It was not large but was strongly built. With a hammer he found lying on a shelf, he pried up one of the top boards. He struck another match and peered into the box. Inside, wrapped in sacking, was a lot of the same ore he had found in the leather bag under the skeleton of Jim Kurland.

He blew out the match, and then pushed the board back in place, hitting it a couple of light taps with the hammer. Then he went out, closed the window, and replaced the pane of glass, using some slivers of wood to hold the pane in place.

Jasper Wald, then, had killed Jim Kurland and found the claim. Or perhaps he had found the claim first. The ore was extremely rich, and he was shipping it a very little at a time, to El Paso, where his brother was probably having it milled.

A slow process, certainly, but it was high-grade ore, and no doubt Wald had made plans to file on the claim when there would be no danger of Kurland's disappearance being linked with the proceedings. Everyone from the Forks to the Stone Tree Desert and Agua Dulce Cañon knew Kurland was the only mining man around and also that he regularly penetrated the badlands of the Stone Tree.

The Sandy Kid took to the trail and put the roan to a fast trot. He was foolish, he told himself, to be mixing into something that was no concern of his. It would have been wiser to forget what he had seen after he came out of that crack in the mountain. Even now, he reflected, it was not too late to travel to some far-off place like the Blue Mountains or maybe that Grand Cañon country of Arizona, which he had never seen but had heard cowhands lying about.

Little as he knew about gold, he could tell that the ore he had seen was fabulously rich, for the rock had been lined and threaded with it, and being so heavy it had to be rich ore. Such a boxful as he had seen in the express office might be worth two or three thousand dollars.

Now that he thought about it, he had an idea where that claim was located. Not more than a half mile from where he had jumped into the crack to escape the steer, the plateau broke sharply off in a sheer cliff, some fifty or sixty feet high, that overhung the waterless, treeless waste of Stone Tree Desert and could even open upon the desert itself. That rupture, obviously the result of volcanic disturbance, could have exposed the vein from which the ore had come.

Pure speculation, of course, but the Sandy Kid had an idea he was nosing along the right trail. Also, he was aware that his interest did not arise from chivalry. He was not going into this to help a lady in distress. Trouble with Jasper Wald and his two hardbitten henchmen was not lightly to be invited, and, if he did go into it knowing what he was facing, it was only partly because of the way Betty Kurland had looked at him that he was following through.

It was a fool thing, he told himself. He had no particular urge to get money. Much as he'd like a ranch, he didn't want to have his head shot off getting it. He admitted to himself that, if it had not been for Betty, he would never have gone all the way into this fight.

"The devil with it!" he said viciously. "I'll go back to the Bar W and roll my soogan and hit the trail!"

But when he came to the last forks, he kept on toward the mountains. He circled when he hit the willows and let the pony take its own gait. He was just edging out toward the cliff edge where he could see over into the Stone Tree when a rifle bullet hit the fork of his saddle with a wicked thwack, and then the bullet whined off ahead of him. It was a wonder it hadn't glanced back into his stomach or hit the pony's head.

The echo of the report drifted over him as he hit the ground running, and he grabbed the bridle and swung the bay pony back into the brush. Then he slid his Winchester .44 out of the saddle scabbard and crawled like an Indian toward the cliff edge. That shot meant that somebody wasn't fooling, so the Kid wasn't planning on fun himself. He was some shakes with a Winchester, and, when he got to cover where he could see out, he looked around, trying to locate the spot the varmint had shot from. There was nobody in sight.

The Sandy Kid was not a trusting soul. His past dealings with Comanches had not been calculated to inspire any confidence in the serene and untrammeled appearance of woods or mountains. So, after a long look, he left the bay pony tethered to a bush and crawled to the very lip of the cliff. When he glanced over, he could see something that looked like a pile of waste and rock taken from a mine tunnel, but he wasn't looking for that. All in good time he could have an interest in the gold.

Then, in the rocks farther along the rim of the cliff, he detected a slight movement. He looked again, widening and then squinting his eyes. It looked like a boot heel. Not much of a mark at that distance, and not much damage could be done if he hit it.

We'll scare the daylights out of you, anyway, he thought, and, lifting the Winchester, he nestled his cheek affectionately against the stock and squeezed off a shot.

Dust obscured the spot for a moment, but no dust could blot out the startled yell he heard. Somebody lunged into view then, and the Sandy Kid's jaw dropped. It was Betty Kurland! She was wearing a man's trousers and a man's shirt and limping with one boot heel gone, but that hair could belong to nobody else.

He got up, waving his arms, and ran out to meet her. She turned on him, and her own rifle was coming hip high when she got a better look and recognized him. She came on a couple of steps, and then stopped, her eyes flashing with indignation.

"I thought you were my friend!" she flared at him. "Then you shoot at me!"

"You shot at me!" he declared. "How was I to know?"

"That's different!"

Such feminine logic was so amazing that he gulped and swallowed. "You shouldn't have come out here," he protested. "It isn't safe!"

"I wanted to find my father," she said. "Where is he?"

He led her to the lip of the cliff, and they found a way down. The Kid wanted a look at that desert, first. They came around in full sight of the mine tunnel and were just in time to see a man climbing out of a hole.

"I'll go get what's left of Kurland," they heard the man say. "They'll never find him here."

The Sandy Kid was cursing softly, for he had been so preoccupied with the girl that he had walked around unthinking and now found himself looking into a gun held by Jasper Wald. The rancher had seen him, even if Jack Swarr, climbing from the freshly dug grave, had not.

"Well, now," Wald said. "If this ain't nice. You and that girl walkin' right up on us."

"Don't you try nothing," the Kid said. "This girl is known to be here. If she doesn't show up, you'll have the law around."

Wald chuckled. "No, we won't. Not for long, anyway. I'll just tell them this Kurland girl showed up to meet you, and you two took off to get married, over to Lordsburg or somewheres. They'll figger you eloped and never even think of lookin' for you."

Swarr grinned. "Hey, that's a good idea, boss. An' we can pile 'em in the same hole with her pa."

"If I were you," the Sandy Kid said, "I'd guess again. I just come from Argo Springs. I know all about that gold ore you've been shipping to El Paso, and I ain't the only one."

Jasper Wald hesitated. His idea for getting rid of the two had been a sudden inspiration and a good one, but the thought that the Kid might have mentioned the gold to someone in Argo Springs disturbed him. It would mean he would have to move slowly, or worse, that he was already suspected.

Suddenly there was a clatter of stones, and they looked up. Only Wald, who held the gun on the Kid, did not shift his eyes. The newcomer was Dutch Schweitzer.

"Watch that *hombre*, boss," the German said hoarsely. "He's a gunslick."

"Him?" Swarr was incredulous. "That kid?"

"How old was Bill Bonney?" Dutch asked sarcastically. "He flashed a gun on me today so fast I never even saw his hand move."

Angered and worried, Jasper Wald stared at the Kid.

"Listen, boss," Dutch said, "he's lyin'. I nosed around town after he left. After he left me, I mean. He never talked to nobody."

"How did I find out about the gold in that box you brought in? Addressed to Henry Wald in El Paso?" the Kid asked him.

"He must have seen the box," Dutch protested.

The Sandy Kid's mind was running desperately ahead, trying to find a way out. "Also" he added, "I checked on this claim. You never filed on it, so I did."

"What?" Wald's shout was a bellow of fury. His face went dark with blood. "You filed on this claim? Why, you . . ." Rage drove all caution from his mind. "I'll shoot you, blast you, and let you die right out in the sun! You . . ."

"Boss!" Swarr shouted. "Hold it! Mebbe he's lyin'! Mebbe he didn't file! Anyway," he added craftily, "why kill him until he signs the claim over to us?"

Wald's rage died. He glanced at Swarr. "You're right," he said. "We can get possession that way."

The Sandy Kid chuckled. "You'll have no cinch getting me to sign anything."

"It'll be easy," Wald said sharply. "We'll just start by tyin' up that girl and takin' her boots off. By the time she gets a little fire on her feet, you'll sign."

Dutch Schweitzer glanced at his chief. Then he helped Jack Swarr tie the girl. Swarr knelt and pulled off her boots. He drew deeply on his cigarette and thrust it toward her foot.

Dutch stared at them, his eyes suddenly hardening. "None of that," he said. "I thought you were bluffin'. Cut it out!"

"Bluffin'?" Swarr looked up. "I'll show you if I'm bluffin'!" He jammed the cigarette forward, and Betty screamed.

Dutch Schweitzer's face went pale, and with an oath he grabbed for a gun. At the same time, Jasper Wald swung his gun toward the German. That was all the break the Sandy Kid needed. His right hand streaked for his gun butt, and he was shooting with the first roar from Wald's gun.

The Kid's first shot took Jack Swarr in the stomach as the big man lunged upward, clawing for his pistol. Dutch had a gun out and was firing. The Kid saw his body jerk with the impact of Wald's bullet, and he swung his own gun. Wald faced him at the same instant.

For one unbelieving instant, the Sandy Kid looked over the stabbing flame of his own Colt into the flaring muzzle of Wald's six-shooter. He triggered his gun fast at almost point-blank range.

He swayed on his feet, his legs spread wide, and saw Jasper Wald's cruel face turn white before his eyes. The rancher's knees sagged, and he went to the ground, glaring bitterly at the Sandy Kid. He tried then to lift his gun, but the Kid sprang forward and knocked it from his grasp. Wald slumped over on the sand, his face contorted.

Swarr, the Kid saw at a glance, was dead. Yet it had not been only his bullet, for the German must have got in at least one shot. Swarr's face and head were bloody.

Schweitzer lay on his back, his face upturned to the sun. The Sandy Kid knelt beside him, but a glance told him there was nothing he or anyone could do.

Dutch stared at him. "Never was no hand to abuse women," he said, "never . . . no hand."

The Sandy Kid turned to Betty Kurland, and quickly untied her.

"Let's get out of here," the Kid said. Taking her by the hand, he led her toward the path down which Schweitzer had come.

On the cliff top, they stood for a moment together. Betty's face was white now, and her eyes seemed unusually large and dark. He noticed then that she hadn't limped.

"Was your foot burned badly?" he asked. "I didn't think to help you."

"It wasn't burned at all," she told him. "I jerked my foot back as he thrust the cigarette at it."

"But you screamed?" he protested.

"Yes, I know," she said, looking at him. "You had to have your chance to draw, and they hadn't taken away your gun. And I knew about Dutch Schweitzer."

"Knew about him? What?"

"The Apaches killed his wife. They burned her. I thought, maybe that was why he drank so much, I guess."

When they were on the trail toward the Forks, he looked at her and then glanced quickly away. "Well, you've got your claim," he said. "All you've got to do is stake it out and file on it. I never did. You found your pa, too. Looks like you're all set. I reckon I'll hug the rawhide and head out of the country. A loose horse is always hunting new pastures."

"I'll need a good man to ramrod that mine for me," she protested. "Wouldn't you do that? I promised you half, too."

"Ma'am" — the Sandy Kid was growing red around the gills and desperate, for she was sure enough a pretty girl — "I reckon I never was made to stay no place. I'm packing my duffel and taking the trail out of here. If anybody comes around asking for the Sandy Kid, you tell 'em he lit a shuck and went to Texas."

He turned his horse at the forks of the road and headed for the Bar W. His own horse was there, and, since Wald wouldn't be needing this bay pony, he might need him out West there, Arizona way. He sure did aim to see that Grand Cañon down which flowed the Colorado. A mile deep, they said. Of course, that was a durned lie, but she might be pretty deep, at that.

Once, he glanced back over his shoulder. The girl was only a dim figure on the skyline.

"First thing we know," he said to the bay pony, "she'd have me a-setting in church a-wearing a fried shirt. I'd shore be halter broke."

The bay pony switched his tail and picked up its feet in an Indian trot, and the Sandy Kid broke into song, a gritty baritone that made the bay lay back its ears.

Oh, there was a young cowhand
who used to go riding,
There was a young cowhand
named Johnny Go-day!
He rode a black pony an' never was lonely,
For a girl never said to him Johnny, go 'way!

The Nester and the Paiute

He was riding loose in the saddle when we first saw him, and he was wearing a gun, which was some unusual for the Springs these days. Out on the range where a man might have a run-in with a locoed steer or maybe a rattler, most of the boys carried guns, but around town Sheriff Todd had sort of set up a ruling against it. It was the second time I'd seen him, but he looked some different this morning, and it took me a minute or two to decide what it was made the difference, and then I decided it was partly the gun and partly that look in his eyes.

He reined in that yellow horse in front of Green's and hooked one long leg around the saddle horn.

"Howdy."

"Howdy." Hatcher was the only one who answered; only the rest of us sort of looked up at him. He dug in his shirt pocket for the makings and started to build a smoke.

Nobody said anything, just sort of waiting to see what was on his mind. He had an old carbine in a saddle scabbard, and the scabbard wasn't under his leg, but with the muzzle pointed down and the stock close to his hand. A man riding thataway ain't rightly figuring on using a rope on no stock. That rifle would be in the way, but if he was figuring on needing a rifle right quick, it would be a plumb handy way to carry it.

When he had his smoke built, he lit it with his left hand, and I got a good glimpse of his eyes, kind of cold and gray, and them looking us over.

Nobody here was friendly to him, yet nobody was unfriendly, neither. All of us had been around the Springs for years, all but him. He was the nester from Squaw Rock, and nesters aren't right popular around cow range. However, the times was a-changing and we all knew it, so it wasn't like it might have been a few years before, when the country was new.

"Seen a tall *hombre* on a black horse?"

He asked the question like maybe it was a formality that he wanted to get over with, and not like he expected an answer.

"What sort of man?"

It was Hatcher who had started the talking as if he was riding point for the rest of us.

"Maybe two hundred pounds, sort of limp in his right leg, maybe. Rides him a black horse, long-gaited critter, and he wears two guns, hanging low."

"Where'd you see him?"

"Ain't never see him. I've seen his sign."

Yanell, who lived over nigh to Squaw Rock himself, looked up from under his hat brim and spat into the dust. What he was thinking we all were thinking. If this nester read sign that well and trailed the Paiute clean from Squaw Rock, he was no pilgrim.

That description fitted the Paiute like a glove, and nobody amongst us had any love for the Paiute. He'd been living in the hills over toward White Hills for the last six years, ever since he came back to the country after his trouble. The Paiute had done a bit of horse stealing and rustling from time to time and we all knew it, but none of us was right anxious to trail him down. Not that we were afraid. Only, none of us had ever caught him in the act, so we just left it up to Sheriff Todd, who wanted it that way. This here nester seemed to have some ideas of his own.

"No," Hatcher said, "I ain't seen nobody like that. Not lately."

The nester — his name was Bin Morley — nodded like he'd expected nothing else. "Reckon I'll ride along," he said. "Be seeing you."

He swung his leg back over the saddle and kicked his toe into a stirrup. The yellow horse started to walk like it was a signal for something, and we sat there watching him fade out down toward the cottonwoods at the end of the town.

Hatcher bit off a hunk of chewing and rolled it in his jaws. "If he meets up with the Paiute," he said, "he's asking for trouble."

Yanell spat into the dust. "Reckon he'll handle it," he said dryly. "Somethin' tells me the Paiute rustled cows off the wrong *hombre*."

"Wonder what Sheriff Todd'll say?" Hatcher wanted to know.

"This here Morley, now," Yanell said, "he sort of looks like a man who could do his own lawin'. He's one of them *hombres* what ain't felt the civilizin' influences of Sheriff Todd's star, nor he ain't likely to."

The nester's yellow horse ambled casually out over the trail toward White Hills. From time to time Bin Morley paused to study the trail, but from here it was much easier. He knew the look of the big black's track now, and, from what was said later, I reckon the Paiute wasn't really expecting any trouble. Me, I was plumb curious. My pappy always did tell me my bump of curiosity was too big for my britches, but after a few minutes I got up off the porch and walked around to where my steel-dust was standing, three-legged, in the dust. I threw a leg over him and trailed out after the nester.

Maybe I'd been listening too much to the old-timers around telling of cattle drives and Indian fighting. You listen to the stories a mite and you get to honing to see some of them fracases yourself.

Now I knew the Paiute. Actually he was only part Paiute, and the rest was some brand of white, but, whatever it was, the combination had resulted in pure poison. That was one reason everybody was plenty willing to accept Sheriff Todd's orders to leave law enforcement to him. I will say, he did a good job. He did a good job until it came to the Paiute.

It was understandable about the Paiute. That Indian left no more trail than a snake going over a flat rock, and no matter how much we suspected, nobody could ever get any evidence on him. Sheriff Todd had been on his trail a dozen times, but each time he lost it. I knew what Yanell was thinking just as well as if it was me. Anybody who could trail the Paiute plumb from Squaw Creek wasn't likely to holler calf rope for any

Indian rustler without smoking things up a mite. Me, I was just curious enough and ornery enough to want to see what would happen when this nester cornered the Paiute.

He was a big, sullen brute, the Paiute was. Rumor had it he'd killed a half dozen men, and certainly there were several that started out hunting him that never showed up until somebody found 'em dead, but there'd never been evidence to prove a thing. He could sling a gun, and, when we had the turkey shoot around about Thanksgiving, he used to fetch his guns down, and nine times out of ten he got himself a turkey — and he used a six-gun. You take a man that moves around over the hills like a ghost, Indian footing it over the rocks and through the brush, and who shoots like that, and you get an idea why anybody was worried about getting him in a corner.

Six miles out I got a glimpse of the nester. The yellow horse was ambling along, taking it easy in a sort of loose-jointed trot that didn't look like much but seemed to eat up the country right fast.

The day wore on and I kept to the brush, not knowing how Morley would take it if he knew I was trailing him. Then all of a sudden I saw him swing the yellow horse off the trail and drop to the ground. He was there for a minute, and, riding closer, I could see he was bending over the body of a man. Then he swung back into the saddle and moseyed off down the trail.

When he went over the next rise, I turned my horse down the hill. Even before I rode up, I knew who the dead man was. I could see his horse lying in the cactus off to one side, and only one man in that country rode a bay with a white splash on the shoulder. It was Sheriff Todd.

There was a sign around, but I didn't need more than a glance at it to tell me what had happened. Sheriff Todd had run into the Paiute unexpected-like and caught him flat-footed with stolen stock, the first time he had ever had that chance. Only from the look of it, Todd had been caught flat-footed himself. His gun was out, but unfired, and he had been shot twice in the stomach.

Looking down at that body, I felt something change inside me. I knew right then, no matter how the nester came out, I was going to follow on my own hook. For Sheriff Todd was still alive when he hit the ground, and that Paiute had bent over him, put a pistol to the side of his head, and blew half his head off. There were powder burns around that hole in his temple where the bullet went in. It had been cold-blooded murder.

Swinging a leg over that gelding, I was starting off when I happened to think of a gun, and turned back and recovered the one Sheriff Todd had worn. I also got his saddle gun out of the scabbard and started off, trailing the nester.

From now on the sign was bad. The Paiute knew he was up against it now. He was taking time to blot his tracks, and, if it hadn't been for Morley, I'd never have trailed him half as far as I did.

We hadn't gone more than a few miles farther before I saw something that turned me plumb cold inside. The Paiute had turned off at the Big Joshua and was heading down the trail toward Rice Flats. That scared me, because Rice Flats was where my girl lived, down there in a cabin with her kid brother and her ma, and they had lived there alone ever since her dad fell asleep and tumbled off his spring wagon into the cañon. The Paiute had been nosing around the flats long enough to scare Julie some, but I reckon it was the sheriff who had kept him away.

Now Sheriff Todd was gone, and the Paiute knew he was on the dodge from here on. He would know that killing Sheriff Todd was the last straw, and he'd have to get clean out of the country. Knowing that, he'd know he might as well get hung for one thing as another.

As my gelding was a right fast horse, I started him moving then. I jacked a shell into the chamber of the sheriff's carbine and I wasn't thinking much about the nester. Yet by the time I got to the cabin on the flats, I knew I was too late.

My steel-dust came into the yard at a dead run and I hit the dust and went for that house like a saddle tramp for a chuck wagon. I busted inside and took a quick look around. Ma Frank was lying on the bed with a big gash in her scalp, but she was conscious.

"Don't mind me," she said. "Go after that Injun! He has taken off with Julie on her black."

"What about you?" I asked, although goodness knows I was wanting nothing more than to be out and after Julie.

"'Brose'll be back right soon. He rid over to Elmer's after some side meat."

'Brose was short for Ambrose, her fourteen-year-old boy, so knowing he'd be back, I swung a leg over my saddle and headed out for the hills. My steel-dust knew something was in the wind and he hustled his hocks for those hills like he was heading home from a trail drive.

The Paiute had Julie and he was a killing man, a killing man who knew he was up the creek without a paddle now, and, if he was gotten alive, he'd be rope meat for sure. No man ever bothered a woman or killed a man as well liked in that country as Sheriff Todd without riding under a cottonwood limb. Me, I'm a plumb peaceable sort of hand, but when I saw the sheriff back there, I got my dander up. Now that Paiute had stolen my girl and I was a wild man.

Ever see that country out toward the White Hills? God must have been cleaning up the last details of the job when He made that country, and just dumped a lot of the slag and waste down in a lot of careless heaps. Ninety percent of that country stands on end, and what doesn't stand on end is dryer than a salt desert and hotter than a bronco on a hot rock.

The Paiute knew every inch of it, and he was showing us all he knew. We went down across a sun-baked flat where weird dust devils danced like crazy in a world where there was nothing but heat and dust and misery for man and beast. No cactus there, not even salt grass or yeso. Nothing grew there, and the little winds that stirred along the dusty levels made you think of snakes gliding along the ground.

My gelding slowed to a walk and we plodded on, and somewhere miles ahead, beyond the wall of sun-dancing heat waves, there was a column of dust, a thin, smoky trail where the nester rode ahead of me. Right then, I began to have a sight of respect for that long-legged yellow horse he was riding because he kept on going and even gained ground on my steel-dust.

Finally we got out of that hell's valley and took a trail along the rusty edge of some broken rock, winding higher toward some saw-toothed ridges that gnawed at the sky like starving coyotes in a dry season. That trail hung like an eyebrow to the face of the cliff we skirted, and twice, away up ahead, I heard shots. I knew they were shots from the Paiute, because I'd seen that carbine the nester carried. It was a Spencer .56.

Ever seen one? Mister, all they lack is wheels! A caliber .56 with a bore like a cannon, and them shooting soft-nosed lead bullets. What they do to a man ain't pretty, like you'll know. I knew well enough it wasn't the nester shooting because when you unlimber a Spencer .56, she has a bellow like a mad bull in a rock cañon.

Sundown came, and then the night, and little breezes picked up and blew, cool and pleasant, down from the hills. Stop? There was no time for stopping. I knew my gelding would stand anything the Paiute's horse would, and I knew by the shooting that the Paiute knew the nester was on his trail. He wasn't going to get ary a chance to cool his heels with that nester tailing him down them draws and across the level bunch grass.

97

The Paiute? I wasn't worried so much about Julie now. He might kill her, but that I doubted as long as he had a prayer of getting away with her. He was going to have to keep moving or shoot it out.

The longer I rode, the more respect I got for Bin Morley. He stuck to that Paiute's trail like a cocklebur to a sheep, and that yellow horse of his just kept his head down and kept moseying along those trails like he was born to 'em, and he probably was.

The stars came out and then the moon lifted, and they kept on going. My steel-dust was beginning to drag his heels, and so I knew the end was coming. At that, it was almost morning before it did come.

How far we'd come or where we were I had no idea. All I knew was that up ahead of me was the Paiute with my girl, and I wanted a shot at him. Nobody needed to tell me I was no hand to tie in a gun battle with the Paiute with him holding a six-gun. He was too slick a hand for me.

Then all of a sudden as the sky was turning gray and the hills were losing their shadows, I rounded a clump of cottonwoods and there was that yellow horse, standing three-footed, cropping absently at the first green grass in miles.

The nester was nowhere in sight, but I swung down and, with the carbine in hand, started down through the trees, cat-footing along with no idea what I might see or where they could have gone. Then all of a sudden I came out on the edge of a cliff and looked down at a cabin in a grassy basin, maybe a hundred feet below and a good four hundred yards away.

Standing in front of that cabin were two horses. My face was pretty pale, and my stomach felt sick, but I headed for the trail down, when I heard a scream. It was Julie!

Then, in front of the cabin, I heard a yell, and that durned nester stepped right out in plain sight and started walking up to the cabin, and he wasn't more than thirty yards away from it.

That fool nester knew he was asking for it. The Paiute might have shot from behind the doorjamb or from a window, but maybe the nester figured I was behind him and he might draw him out for my fire. Or maybe he figured his coming out in the open would make him leave the girl alone. Whatever his reason, it worked. The Paiute stepped outside the door.

Me? I was standing up there like a fool, just a-gawking, while there, right in front of my eyes, the Paiute was going to kill a man. Or was he?

He was playing big Indian right then. Maybe he figured Julie was watching or maybe he thought the nester would scare. Mister, that nester wouldn't scare a copper cent.

The Paiute swaggered about a dozen steps out from the cabin and stood there, his thumbs in his belt, sneering. The nester, he just moseyed along kind of lazy-like, carrying his old Spencer in his right hand like he'd plumb forgot about his hand gun.

Then, like it was on a stage, I seen it happen. That Paiute went for his guns and the nester swung up his Spencer. There were two shots — then a third.

It's a wonder I didn't break my neck getting down that trail, but when I run up, the Paiute was lying there on his back with his eyes glazing over. I took one look and then turned away, and you can call me a pie-eating tenderfoot, but I was sick as I could be. Mister, did you ever see a man who'd been hit by two soft-nosed .56-caliber bullets? In the stomach?

Bin Morley came out with Julie, and I straightened up, and she ran over to me and began asking how Ma was. She wasn't hurt none, as the nester got there just in time.

We took the horses back, and then I fell behind with the nester. I jerked my head toward the Paiute's body.

"You going to bury him?" I asked.

He looked at me like he thought I was soft in the head.

"What for? He picked the place himself, didn't he?"

We mounted up.

"Besides," he said, "I've lost two whole days as it is, and getting behind on my work ain't going to help none." He was stuffing something in his slicker on the back of his horse.

"What's that?" I asked.

"A ham," he said grimly, "a whole ham. I brought it clean from Tucson, an' that durned Paiute stole it off me. Right out of my cabin. Ma, she was out picking berries when it happened."

"You mean," I said, "you trailed the Paiute clean over here just for a ham?"

"Mister" — the nester spat — "you're durned right I did! Why, Ma and me ain't et no hawg meat since we

100

left Missouri, coming three year ago." The steel-dust started to catch up with Julie's pony, but I heard the nester saying: "Never was no hand to eat beef, nohow. Too durned stringy. Gets in my teeth!"

Barney Takes a Hand

Blinding white sun simmered above the thick, flour-like dust of the road, and the ragged mesquite beside the trail was gray with that same dust. Between the ranch and the distant purple hills, there was nothing but endless flats and sagebrush, dusty and dancing with heat waves.

Tess Bayeux stood in the doorway and shaded her eyes against the sun. The road was empty, empty to the horizon beyond which lay the little cow town of Black Mesa. With a little sigh of hopelessness, she turned away. It was too soon. Even if Rex Tilden had received her note and decided to come, he could never come so quickly.

After an hour, during which she forced herself not to look even once, she returned to the door. The road was still empty, only white dust and heat. Then her eyes turned the other way, and she looked out across the desert, out to where the road dwindled off to a miserable trail into the badlands where nothing lived. For an instant then, she thought the heat played tricks with her eyes, for between her and the distant cliffs was a tiny figure.

Struck by curiosity, she stood in the doorway, watching. She was a slender girl with a pert, impudent little nose above a friendly mouth and lips that laughed when her eyes did.

She was still there, much later, when the figure took shape and became a man. The man wore no hat. His shaggy black hair was white with dust, his heavy woolen shirt was open at the neck, and his hairy chest was also dusty.

The man's face was unshaven, and his jaw was heavy, almost brutal under the beard and dust. The jeans he wore were strange to the cow country, and his feet wore the ragged remains of what had been sneakers. His jeans were belted with a wide leather belt, curiously carved. He wore no gun.

Several times the man staggered, and finally, when he turned from the road and stopped at the gate, he grasped the top with his big hands and stared at Tess Bayeux.

For a long time he stared while she tried to find words, and then one of the big hands dropped and he fumbled for the latch. He came through the gate and closed it behind him. It was a small thing, yet in his condition it told her something.

The man came on toward the house, and, when she saw his face, she caught her breath. Sunburn had cracked the skin until it had bled, and the blood had dried. The face was haggard, a mask of utter weariness from which only the eyes glowed and seemed to be alive.

Brought to herself suddenly, she ran inside for water. She tried to pick up the dipper, but dropped it. Then she carried the bucket to the man, and he seized it in his two big hands and lifted it to his mouth. She put out a hand to stop him, but he had merely taken a mouthful and then held it away, sloshing the water about in his mouth.

He looked at her wisely, and suddenly she had a feeling that this man knew everything, that he was afraid of nothing, that he could do anything with himself. She knew how his whole body must be crying for water, yet he knew the consequences of too much too soon and held the bucket away, his face twisted as though in a sneer at his fervid desire for its cool freshness.

Then he swallowed a little, and for a moment his face twisted again. He straightened it with an effort and, picking up the wash basin beside the door, filled it, and began to bathe his face and hands slowly, tenderly. In all this time he said nothing, made no explanation.

A long time ago Tess had ridden with her brother into the badlands beyond the desert. It was a waterless horror, a nightmare of gigantic stones and gnarled cacti, a place where nothing lived. How far had this man come? How could he have walked all that distance across the desert? That he had walked was obvious, for his sneakers were in tatters and there was some blood on the ground where he stood.

He shook the water from his eyes and then, without speaking, stepped up on the porch and entered the house. Half frightened, she started to speak, but he merely stretched out upon the floor in the cool interior and almost at once was asleep.

Again she looked at the road. And still it was empty. If Rex Tilden were to come in time, he must come soon. Judge Barker had told her that as long as she had possession, there was a chance. If she lost possession before he returned from Phoenix, there was little chance that anything could be done.

It was sundown when she saw them coming. It was not Rex Tilden, for he would come alone. It was the others.

It was Harrington and Clyde, the men Tess feared. They rode into the yard at a canter and reined in at the edge of the verandah.

"Well, Miss Bayeux" — George Clyde's silky voice was underlined with malice — "you are ready to leave?"

"No."

Tess stood very still. She knew there was little Clyde wouldn't stoop to if he could gain an end. Harrington was brutal, rough. Clyde was smooth. It was Clyde she feared most, yet Harrington would do the rough work. He was a big man and cruel.

"Then I am afraid we will have to move you," said Clyde. "We have given you time. Now we can give you only ten minutes more to get what you want and get out on the road."

"I'm not going." Tess held her head high.

Clyde's mouth tightened. "Yes, you are. Of course" — he crossed his hands on the saddle horn — "if you want to come to my place, I think I could make you comfortable there. If you don't come to my place, there will be nothing in Black Mesa for you."

"I'll stay here."

Tess stood facing them. She couldn't win. She knew that in her heart. Rex was too late now, and the odds were against her. Still, where would she go? She had no money; she had no friends who dared help her. There had been only Tilden.

"All right, Harrington," Clyde said grimly. "You move her. Put her outside the gate."

Harrington swung down from the saddle, his face glistening with evil. He stepped up on the porch.

"Stay where you are!" a voice said from behind her. Tess started. She had forgotten the stranger, and his voice was peculiar. It was low, ugly with some fierceness that was only just covered by an even tone. "You come a step farther and I'll kill you," he said.

Harrington stood flat-footed. George Clyde was quicker.

"Tess Bayeux, who is this man?"

"Shut up!" The man walked out on the porch, and his feet were cat-like in their movements. "And get moving."

"Listen, my friend," Clyde said, "you're asking for trouble. You're a stranger here and you don't know what you're saying."

"I know a skunk by the smell." The stranger advanced to the edge of the porch, and his red-rimmed eyes glared at Clyde. "Get going!"

"Why, you . . ."

Harrington reached for him.

He reached, but the stranger's left hand shot out and seized Harrington by the throat and jerked him to his tiptoes. Holding him there, the stranger slapped him twice across the face. Slapped him only, but left him with a trickle of blood at the corner of his mouth. Then, setting him down on his heels, the stranger shoved, and big Deek Harrington sprawled at full length in the dust.

Clyde's face was deadly. He glanced at Harrington, and then at the stranger, and then his hand shot for his gun. But the stranger was quicker. He seized the bridle and jerked the horse around and, catching Clyde by his gun arm, whipped him from the saddle to throw him into the dust.

Clyde's gun flew free, and the stranger caught it deftly and thrust it into his own waistband.

"Now," he said, "start walking. When you're over the horizon, I'll turn your horses loose. Until then, walk!"

Harrington staggered to his feet, and Clyde got up more slowly. His black coat was dusty. The stranger looked at Harrington.

"You still wear a gun," he said coolly. "Want to die? If you do, why don't you try drawing it?"

Harrington wet his lips. Then his eyes fell and he turned away.

"That goes for later," the stranger said. "If you want to try a shot from up the road, do it. I haven't killed a snake in a week."

The two men stumbled from the yard, and the stranger stood there, watching them go. Then he picked up the bucket and drank, for a long time. When the two recent visitors were growing small toward the horizon, he turned the horses loose, hitting each a ringing slap on the haunches.

They would never stop short of town if he knew Western horses.

"I'm going to get supper," Tess told him. "Would you like to eat?"

"You know I would." He looked at her for a moment. "Then you can tell me what this is all about."

Tess Bayeux worked swiftly, and, when she had the coffee on and the bacon frying, she turned to look at the man who had come to her rescue. He was slumped in a chair at the table. Black hair curled in the V of his shirt, and there was black hair on his forearms.

"You aren't a Western man?" she asked him.

"I was . . . once," he answered, "but that was a long time ago. I lived in Texas, in Oklahoma, then in Utah. Now I'm back in the West to stay."

"You have a home somewhere?"

"No. Home is where the heart is, they say, and my heart is here" — he touched his chest — "for now. I'm still a dreamer, I reckon. Still thinking of the one girl who is somewhere."

"You've had a hard time," she said, looking at him again.

She had never seen so much raw power in a man, never seen so much sleeping strength as in the muscles that rolled beneath his shirt.

"Tell me about you," he said. "Who are them two men that were here?"

"Harrington and Clyde," she told him. "The H and C Cattle Company. They moved in here two years ago, during the drought. They bought land and cattle. They prospered. They aren't big, but then nobody else is, either.

"The sheriff doesn't want trouble. Clyde outtalks those who dislike him. My father did, very much, and he wasn't outtalked. He died, killed by a fall from a bad horse, about a year ago. It seems he was in debt. He was in debt to Nevers, who runs the general store in Black Mesa. Not much, but more than he could pay. Clyde bought up the notes from Nevers.

"Wantrell, a lawyer in Phoenix who knew my father, is trying to get it arranged so we will have water here. If we do, we could pay off the notes in a short time. If we had water, I could borrow money in Prescott. There is water on government land above us, and that's why Clyde wants it. He tried to get me to move away for the notes. Then he offered to pay me five hundred dollars and give me the notes.

"When I refused, he had some of his men dam the stream and shut off what water I had. My cattle died. Some of my horses were run off. Then he came in with some more bills and told me I'd have to leave or pay. He has some sort of a paper on the place. It says that my father promised to give Nevers the place if he didn't pay up or if anything happened to him."

"No friends?" asked the man.

"Yes, a man named Rex Tilden," Tess said. "He rode for Dad once and then started a ranch of his own. He's good with a gun, and, when I wrote to him, he said he would come. He's five days late now."

The stranger nodded. "I know." He took a small wallet from his pocket. "That his?"

She caught it up, her face turning pale. She had seen it many times.

"Yes! You know him? You have seen him?"

"He's dead. Drygulched. He was killed near Santos three days ago."

"You knew him?" Tess repeated.

"No. I got kicked off a train I was riding. I found him dying. He told me about you, asked me to help. There was nobody else around, so I came."

"Oh, thank you! But Rex! Rex Tilden dead. And because of me!"

His face didn't change. "Mebbe." He brought out the gun he had taken from Clyde and checked it. "Mebbe need this. Where's that dam?"

"Up there, on the ridge. But they have it guarded."

"Do they?" He didn't look interested.

She put the bacon on his plate and poured coffee. He ate in silence, and, when he had finished, it was dark. He got up suddenly.

"You got a gun?" he asked.

"Just a small rifle, for rabbits."

"Use it. If anything moves, shoot."

"But it might be you," she protested. "When you come back, I mean."

He smiled, and his whole face seemed to lighten. "When anything moves, shoot. It won't be me. When I come back, you won't hear me."

"Who are you?" It was the first time she had asked that.

He hesitated, looking at the ground, and then at her, and his eyes glinted with humor. "My name is Barney Shaw," he said then. "That mean anything to you?"

She shook her head.

"Should it?"

"No, I reckon not."

He ate for a while in silence, and then looked up at her.

"A few years ago I was punching cows. Then I worked in the mines. A man saw me in a fight once and trained me. In two years I was one of the best. Then I killed a man in a dice game and got two years for it. He was cheating. I accused him. He struck at me. When the two years were up . . . I'd been sentenced to ten, but they let me out after two . . . I went to sea. I was at sea for four years. Then I decided to come back and find a place for myself, here in the West. But first, a job."

Tess looked at him understandingly. "I need a man," she said, "but I haven't the money to pay."

He looked at his plate. "How about a working share?"

"All right. Fifty-fifty." She smiled ruefully. "But it isn't much. I think Clyde will win, after all."

"Not if I can help it. How much do you owe?"

"A thousand dollars. It might as well be a million. We don't have more than fifty head of cattle on the place, and only four saddle horses."

He went out the back door and vanished. Or so it seemed. Tess, glancing out a moment later, could see nothing. She should have told him about Silva, the guard at the dam. Silva was a killer and quick as a snake.

She turned again to the house and began putting things in order. First, she barricaded the front door, and then opened the window a slit at the bottom. She got out her rifle, checked it, and laid out some ammunition.

Barney Shaw had seen the draw when he had approached the house by the road, so when he left the house, he hit it fast. It was deep enough by a head, and he started away. Fortunately it led toward the dam. It was the old streambed.

From the shadow of a gigantic boulder, he looked up at the dam. Largely brush, logs, and earth, it was a hasty job and homemade. He watched for twenty minutes before he saw the guard. Silva, a Mexican, had found a place for himself where he could command all the approaches to the dam.

In the moonlight, a rock cedar made a heavy shadow. Barney Shaw moved, and then, as Silva's head moved, he froze. He was out in the open, but he knew the light was indistinct. For a long time he stood still, and then, as Silva's head moved again, Shaw glided forward to the shelter of the rock cedar.

He was no more than a dozen feet from the guard now, and through a hole in the bushy top of the cedar he could see Silva's long, lantern jaw, and even the darkness seemed to mark the thin mustache the man wore.

When Silva stood up, Shaw could see that the man was tall, yet feline in his movements. Silva stretched, and then turned and came toward the cedar, walking carelessly. He had put his rifle aside and walked with the aimlessness of a man without care. Yet something in that very carelessness struck Shaw as the guard moved closer.

Silva stepped past the tree, and then whirled and dived straight at Shaw, his knife flashing in the moonlight!

Only that sense of warning saved Barney Shaw. He stepped back, just enough, and whipped a left hook for Silva's chin. It landed, a glancing blow, and the Mexican dropped. But cat-like he was on his feet, and, teeth bared, he lunged again. Shaw stepped in, warding off the knife, and slashed with the edge of his hand for the Mexican's neck. The blow was high and took the man across the temple and ear.

Silva went to his knees and lost his hold on the knife. Barney stepped in, and, as the Mexican came up, he hit him once, twice. The blows cracked like whips in the still air, and the guard dropped to his face.

Dragging him roughly into the open, Shaw hastily bound him hand and foot. Then he walked over and picked up the guard's rifle. It was a Winchester and a good one.

Rustling around, he found an axe and a pick. Without so much as a glance toward the guard, he dropped down the face of the dam and, setting himself, sank the axe into one of the key posts. When he had cut through the posts and the timbers back of them, he was

116

sweating profusely. He was aware, too, that the axe was making a ringing sound that would carry for at least a mile in that still air.

Putting the axe down, he took the pick and began digging at the dirt and rock that were piled up against the water side of the dam. In a few minutes there was a trickle of water coming through, then a fair-size stream.

Carrying the rifle, he went back to the edge of the draw where the timbers had been fitted into notches cut into the rock with a double jack and drill. It took him more than an hour, but he cut two timbers loose.

Dropping his tools, he walked over to look at Silva. The Mexican was conscious, and his eyes blazed when Shaw looked at him, grinning.

"Don't worry," Barney said grimly. "You're safe up here, and, when the dam goes out, they'll be up here in a hurry."

He turned and started away, keeping to the shadows of the cedars. And before he had walked a hundred yards, he heard a *whoosh* and then the rustle of rushing water.

It was a small stream, and the water wasn't much, but it would more than fill the pools down below where Tess Bayeux's cattle came to drink.

There was no warning, and he was still some distance from the girl's cabin when he saw a rifle flash. Simultaneously something struck him a terrific blow alongside the head and he tumbled, face downward, into the gravel. He felt his body sliding, head first, and then he lost consciousness.

117

When Barney Shaw opened his eyes, it was daylight.

He tried to move his head, and pain shot through him like a burning iron. For an instant then he lay still, gathering the will to try again. The side of his head and face that was uppermost was caked with dried blood, and his hair was matted with it. That the morning was well along he knew, for his back was hot with sun, and from the feel the sun was high.

Shaw moved his head and, despite the pain, forced himself to his knees. His head swimming, he peered about.

He lay on a rocky hillside. Below him, half hidden by a clump of cedar, and almost two miles away, was the house of Tess Bayeux. At his right he could hear water running, and that meant the stream he had released had not yet been stopped.

His rifle and pistol were still with him. Gingerly he felt his head. It was badly swollen, and the scalp was furrowed by a bullet. He had bled profusely, and he decided that if his drygulchers had looked at him, they had decided the bullet had entered his skull.

What about Tess? Had they thrown her out? Or was she still holding the place? The silence was ominous, and obviously hours had passed.

Whoever had shot him had no doubt left him for dead and had also freed Silva. How many enemies were there? He had no way of knowing, and Tess had told him nothing. Harrington, Silva, and Clyde were three, and, of them all, George Clyde was the most dangerous because he was the most intelligent.

118

From a position behind some boulders and cedar Shaw studied the small ranch house. There was no evidence of activity, nothing to indicate how the tide of battle had gone.

Then a door banged at the house and he saw a man come out, walking toward the corral. He roped two horses, and in a few minutes two riders started off to town. One of them was Silva.

It took Barney Shaw a half hour of painstaking effort to get to the wall of the house without being seen. He edged along to the corner, and then stopped. Cautiously he peered around. Not ten feet away a man was sitting on the edge of the porch, a rifle on his knees.

He was a short man, but square-jawed and tough. As Barney looked, the man put the rifle against the post, took out a pipe, and began to fill it. Shaw made a quick calculation of his chances and decided against it. With Harrington, perhaps. Not this jasper. This *hombre* was different.

Suddenly Barney Shaw saw a slim piece of pipe, and it gave him an idea. Picking it up, he glanced to see if it was clear, and then looked around for some pebbles. He selected a half dozen. In school, too many years ago, he had been an artist with a bean-shooter.

The man on the porch had a beak of a nose that jutted out above his heavy jaw like the prow on a ship. Taking careful aim, Shaw blew the first pebble. It missed.

The man glanced in the direction of the sound where the pebble hit the ground, and then turned back,

119

puffing contentedly at his pipe. Then Barney fired a second pebble.

It was a direct hit. The pebble, fired from the bean-shooter with force, hit him right on the nose.

With a cry of pain, the man leaped to his feet, one hand grasping his nose. His pipe had fallen to the ground.

Instantly Barney was around the corner. The man, holding his nose, his eyes watering, never saw him coming. It was only when Barney, picking up the rifle, knocked it against the porch that the man whirled about. And Shaw slapped him alongside the head with the butt of the rifle, swinging it free-handed.

The fellow went down, grabbing for his gun, but Shaw stepped in and kicked it from his hand. Then, as the fellow started to rise, Shaw slapped him across the temple with a pistol barrel. The man went down and out.

Coolly Barney shouldered the fellow and, walking with him to the barn, tied him securely and dropped him into a feed bin. Then he went outside and roped a horse. When it was saddled, he led it to the house, left it ground-hitched, and took a quick look. There was no sign of Tess Bayeux. Hiding the extra rifle, he swung into the saddle and started at a canter for town.

He was a tough-looking figure when he rode into town. His shock of black hair was still thick with dust, and his face was stained with blood. The two pistols were thrust into his waistband, and he carried a rifle in his hands. He was cantering up the street when he saw Silva.

The Mexican had come to the door of the saloon, and, when he saw Barney, he swore and dropped a hand for a gun. Shaw swung the rifle and fired across the pommel of the saddle.

The first shot knocked the gun from Silva's hand, the second slammed him back into the wall. It was a shoulder shot. Silva stood there, staring stupidly.

Swinging down, Barney tied the horse and walked along the boardwalk. A dozen people had rushed out at the sound of a shot, but he ignored them. He merely walked to Silva and stopped. For a long time he looked at him.

"Next time I'll kill you," he said, and walked inside.

Three men were in the bar besides the bartender. One of them was a powerfully built man with big hands and a flat nose. Behind the bar were some photos of him, posed like a boxer.

"You a fighter?" Shaw demanded. "If you are, I can lick you."

The man looked at him, his eyes hard.

"I fight for money," he said.

"So do I," Shaw said. He looked at the bartender. "I'll fight this *hombre*, winner take all, skin-tight kid gloves, to a finish."

The bartender's face whitened, and then turned red. "You know who this is?" he demanded. "This is the Wyoming Slasher."

"All right. Line up the fight." Shaw hesitated. "One thing . . . it must be one thousand dollars for the purse."

The bartender laughed. "You'll get that, easy. If you win. The boys like to see the Slasher fight."

Barney Shaw nodded and walked out.

"Who was that?" Harrington demanded as he burst in from the back room. "Who was that man?"

"Some gent with his face all bloody, dusty as sin, wantin' to fight the Slasher for a thousand dollars."

"The Slasher? A thousand dollars?" Harrington's eyes hardened. "Why, I'll fix his clock!"

"No you won't." Clyde walked into the room. "Let it ride. The Slasher will kill him. That will settle everything."

Barney Shaw walked to the hotel, carrying his rifle in the hollow of his arm. He was going up the steps when he saw Tess. Her eyes widened.

"I thought . . . you were dead or gone!" she exclaimed.

"No." He looked at her. "What happened?"

"They surprised me, just before morning. The sheriff was with them, and he made me leave. They had some papers, and they said I had to leave. If I can pay in ten days, I can go back."

"In ten days you'll pay," he promised, and walked past her to the desk. "I want a room and a telegraph blank," he told the clerk.

The clerk shook his head.

"We don't have any rooms."

Barney Shaw reached over the desk and caught the clerk behind the neck and dragged him half over the desk.

122

"You heard me," he said harshly. "I want a room and a telegraph blank. You never sold this hotel out since it was built. Now get me that room."

"Yes, sir." The clerk swallowed and turned the register. "I just remembered. There is a room left."

He put a blank on the desk, and Barney wrote hastily: **Now is the time for all good men to come to the aid of their party.** Then he signed his name. He told the clerk to send the message to the depot and have the agent get it off at once.

Tess came over and stood beside him. "What are you going to do?" she asked.

"Fight the Slasher for a thousand dollars," he said. "That will pay you off."

"The Slasher?" Her face paled. "Oh, not him, Barney. He's awful. He killed a man in a fight. And those men with him. That Dirk Hutchins, McCluskey, and the rest. They are awful."

"Are they?" Barney smiled at her. "I'm going to wash up, then sleep." He turned and walked upstairs.

A man got up from across the room and walked over to the desk.

"What do you think, Martin?" he asked.

Martin Tolliver, the clerk, looked up and his face was grim.

"This one's different, Joe. I'm going to bet on him."

"I think I will, too," Joe said. "But we'll be the only ones."

"Yes," Martin agreed. "But he took hold of me. Joe, that *hombre*'s got a grip like iron. It was like being taken in a vise. I was never so scared in my life."

By noon the day of the fight, cowpunchers were in from the ranches and miners from the mines. The ring had been pitched in the center of the big corral. Martin Tolliver, the hotel clerk, and Joe Todd were betting. They were getting odds.

A little after noon the train came in. By that time everyone was at the corral, waiting for the fight to start, and only Silva saw the men get off the train. There were nine of them who got out of the two passenger coaches. Four were cattlemen, one was a huge, bearded man with blue anchors tatooed on his hands, and the other four were nondescripts in caps and jerseys.

The Wyoming Slasher was first in the ring. He came down, vaulted the ropes, and stood, looking around. His hair was cropped short and he wore a black John L. Sullivan mustache. His eyes were blue and hard, and his face looked like stained oak.

Harrington and another man were in his corner. The sheriff had been selected as the referee.

Barney Shaw came from the hotel, walking across the street wearing an old slicker. As he stepped through the ropes, a stocky man in a checked suit and a black jersey stepped up behind him and put a professional hand on his shoulder.

They got into the ring and walked to the center. The Slasher was half a head taller than Shaw and heavier. His wide cheek bones and beetling brows made him look fierce. The back of his head slid down into a thick neck.

Shaw's hair had been cut, and it was black and curly. He looked brown, and, when he turned and walked to

124

his corner, there was an unexpected lightness in his step.

The Wyoming Slasher dropped his robe, and there was a gasp from the crowd who looked at the rolling muscles of his mighty shoulders and arms. He was built like a wrestler, but his weight was in his gigantic shoulders and deep chest.

He strode to the scratch, skin-tight gloves pulled on. The sheriff motioned, the slicker slid from Barney's shoulders, and he turned and came to scratch. His broad shoulders were powerful and tapered to narrow hips and slim, powerful legs. The Slasher put up his hands and Barney hit him, a quick left that tapped the blood at his thin lips. The Slasher lunged, and Barney slid away, rapping a quick right to the body.

The Slasher strode in, and Barney tried a left to the head that missed, and the Slasher grabbed him by the waist and hurled him to the ground. Shaw lit in a pile of dust, and the sheriff sprang in. "Round!" he shouted.

Shaw walked to his corner.

"He's strong," he said. He waved away the water bottle.

"Them new Queensbury rules would be better for you," his second said out of the corner of his mouth. "London Prize Ring rules was never no good. You hurt a man, and, if he goes down, the round is over."

They started again at the call of time, and Barney walked out quickly. The Slasher rushed, and Barney lanced the fellow's lips with another left, and then stepped around and jabbed with the left again. There was a mix-up. Then Barney stepped away, and the Slasher hit him.

It was a hard right, and it shook Shaw to his heels, but he stepped away. He was skillfully, carefully feeling the bigger man out. Instinctively he knew it would be a hard fight. The other man was like iron, big and very, very strong. It would take time to down him. Barney was trying each punch, trying to find out what the big man would do.

All fighters develop habits. Certain ways of blocking lefts, ducking or countering. By trying each punch a few times Barney Shaw was learning the pattern of the Slasher's fighting, getting a blueprint in his mind.

When the second round had gone four minutes, he took a glancing left to the head and went down, ending the round.

When the minute was up, he went out with a rush. The Slasher put up his hands, and, without even stopping his rush, Barney dropped low and thrust out his left. It caught the Slasher in the midriff and set him back on his heels.

Instantly Barney was upon him. Hitting fast, he struck the Slasher five times in the face with a volley of blows before the bigger man was brought up by the ropes. Then setting himself, he whipped a hard right to the Slasher's ribs.

The crowd was yelling wildly, and the Slasher came off the ropes and swung. Barney went under it and whipped a right to the heart. Then the Slasher's left took him and he rolled over on the ground.

He was badly shaken. In his corner Turkey Tom Ryan, his second, grinned.

"Watch it," he said. "He can hit, the beggar!"

They had wiped the blood from the Slasher's face, and the big man looked hard. Near the Slasher's corner Barney could see George Clyde.

Barney Shaw went up to scratch, and, as the Wyoming Slasher rushed, he stabbed a left to the mouth, parried a left himself, and hit hard to the body. Inside, he hammered away with both hands. He took a clubbing right to the head that cut his forehead and showered him with blood. But suddenly he knew that his time had come, and, instead of backing away, he set himself and began slugging with everything he had.

The Slasher was caught off balance. He tried to get set, but he was too heavy. He struck several ponderous blows, but Barney was knifing his face with those skin-tight gloves. Jabbing a left, he turned his fist as it struck and ripped the Slasher's face. Then he stepped in and threw a wicked uppercut to the body. Then another, and still another. The Slasher started to fall, but Shaw caught him under the chin with the heel of his glove and shoved him erect against the ropes. Stepping back, he smashed both hands to the chin.

With the crowd roaring, Shaw leaped away and the Wyoming Slasher rolled off the ropes and fell flat on his face.

Instantly his seconds were over the ropes and swarming over him. Harrington rushed across the ring and seized one of Barney Shaw's hands, shouting something about his fists being loaded.

127

Turkey Tom shoved him away, and Shaw took off the glove and showed him his bare fist. Harrington snarled something, and Shaw slugged him in the ribs. As the big man started to fall, one of his friends stepped up, and instantly the ring was a bedlam of shouting, fighting men.

It was ten minutes before the ring was cleared, and then the Slasher was able to get to the scratch. He rushed immediately, and Shaw ducked, but, as he ducked, he slipped, and the Slasher hit him and knocked him to his knees. He started to get up, and the Slasher rushed and struck him another ponderous blow. He went down hard. And the round ended.

He was barely on his second's knee when the call of time came again, and, groggy, he went to scratch. The Wyoming Slasher charged. Shaw ducked, went into a clinch, and threw the Slasher with a rolling hip lock. The Slasher went down with a thud.

Still groggy, he came to scratch again, but as they came together, he feinted suddenly. As the Slasher swung, Shaw threw his right, high and hard. It caught the Slasher coming in and knocked him to the ropes. As he rebounded, Shaw hit him with a one-two, so fast the two blows landed with almost the same sound.

The Slasher hit the ground all in one piece and rolled over. After ten minutes he was still unable to stand.

As he shoved to his feet and held there, Harrington suddenly shouted. As one man, his thugs charged the ring and began tearing down the posts.

But even as they charged, the four cattlemen leaped into the ring, as did the man with the blue anchors on his hands. In a breath there was a cordon of men with guns drawn around Barney, around the two stakeholders, and around the shouting Turkey Tom.

Harrington's thugs broke against the flying wedge formed by the cattlemen and Shaw's friends, and the wedge moved on to the hotel.

Tess met them at the door, her eyes wild with anxiety. "You're all right? Oh, I was so afraid. I was sure you'd be hurt."

"You should see the Slasher, ma'am," Turkey Tom said, grinning to show his five gold teeth. "He don't look so good."

"We've got the money to pay off now," Barney told her, smiling. His lips were puffed and there was a blue welt alongside his ear. "We can pay off and start over."

"Yes, and that ain't all!" One of the cattlemen, a big man wearing a black hat, stepped in. "When you wired about the water, I was in Zeb's office. We went to the governor and we got it all fixed up. So I decided it might be a right good idea for me to come up here and get you to feed about five hundred whiteface cows for me . . . on shares."

"She can't," snarled a voice behind them.

As one man they turned. George Clyde stood in the doorway, his lips thinned and his face white.

"She can't, because there's mineral on that place, and I've filed a mining claim that takes in the spring and water source."

His eyes were hard and malicious. Harrington, his face still bloody, loomed behind him. The big man with the anchors on his hands stepped forward and stared hard at Clyde.

"That's him, Sheriff," he said. "The man who killed Rex Tilden."

George Clyde's face stiffened and went white.

"What do you mean?" he shouted. "I was here that night."

"You were in Santos that night. You met Rex Tilden on the road outside of town and shot him. I was up on the hill when it happened and I saw you. You shot him with that Krag Jorgenson rifle. I found one of the shells."

"He's got one of them Krags," the sheriff said abruptly. "I've seen it. He won it from some Danish feller last year in a game of faro. I've never seen another like it."

Barney Shaw had pulled on his trousers over his fighting trunks and slipped on his shirt. He felt the sag of the heavy pistol in his coat pocket and put on the coat. Half turning, he slid the pistol into his waistband.

"That means," he said coolly, "that his mineral claim won't be any use to him. I know he hasn't done any assessment work, and without that he can't hold the claim."

Clyde's eyes narrowed. "You!" he snarled. "If you'd stayed out of this, I'd have made it work. You'll never see me die. And you will never see me arrested!"

Suddenly his hand dropped for his gun, but, even as his hand swept down, Barney Shaw stepped through the crowd, drew, and fired.

Clyde staggered, half turned, and pitched over on his face. Harrington had started to reach, but suddenly he jerked his hand away from his gun as though it were afire.

"I had nothin' to do with no killin'," he said, whining. "I never done nothin'!"

When the sheriff had taken Harrington away, Barney Shaw took Tess by the arm.

"Tess," he asked hesitantly, "does the fifty-fifty deal still go?"

She looked up, her eyes misty and suddenly tender. "Yes, Barney, for as long as you want it."

"Then," he said quietly, "it will be for always."

Man Riding West

Three men were hunkered down by the fire when Jim Gary walked his buckskin up to their camp in the lee of the cliff. The big man across the fire had a shotgun lying beside him. It was the shotgun that made Gary uneasy, for cowhands do not carry shotguns, especially when on a trail drive, as these men obviously were.

Early as it was, the cattle were already bedded down for the night in the meadow alongside the stream, and from their looks they had come far and fast. It was still light, but the clouds were low and swollen with rain.

"How's for some coffee?" Jim asked as he drew up. "I'm riding through, and I'm sure hungry and tuckered."

Somewhere off in the mountains, thunder rolled and grumbled. The fire crackled, and the leaves on the willows hung still in the lifeless air. There were three saddled horses nearby, and among the gear was an old Mother Hubbard-styled saddle with a wide skirt.

"Light an' set up." The man who spoke was lean-jawed and sandy-haired. "Never liked to ride on an empty stomach myself."

More than ever, Gary felt uneasy. Neither of the others spoke. All were tough-looking men, unshaven and dirty, but it was their hard-eyed suspicion that made Jim wonder. However, he swung down and

135

loosened his saddle girth, and then slipped off the saddle and laid it well back under the overhang of the cliff. As he did so, he glanced again at the old saddle that lay there.

The overhang of the cliff was deep where the fire was built for shelter from the impending rain. Jim dropped to an ancient log, gray and stripped of bark, and handed his tin plate over to the man who reached for it. The cook slapped two thick slabs of beef on the plate and some frying-pan bread liberally touched with the beef shavings. Gary was hungry and he dived in without comment, and the small man filled his cup.

"Headed west?" the sandy-haired man asked, after a few minutes.

"Yeah, headed down below the rim. Pleasant Valley way."

The men all turned their heads toward him but none spoke. Jim could feel their eyes on his tied-down guns. There was a sheep and cattle war in the valley.

"They call me Red Slagle. These *hombres* are Tobe Langer and Jeeter Dirksen. We're drivin' to Salt Creek."

Langer would be the big one. "My name's Gary," Jim replied. "Jim Gary. I'm from points yonder. Mostly Dodge and Santa Fe."

"Hear they are hiring warriors in Pleasant Valley."

"Reckon." Jim refused to be drawn, although he had the feeling they had warmed to him since he mentioned heading for the valley.

"Ridin' thataway ourselves," Red suggested. "Want to make a few dollars drivin' cattle? We're short-handed."

"Might," Gary admitted. "The grub's good."

"Give you forty to drive to Salt Creek. We'll need help. From hereabouts the country is plumb rough, an' she's fixin' to storm."

"You've hired a hand. When do I start?"

"Catch a couple of hours' sleep. Tobe has the first ride. Then you take over. If you need help, just you call out."

Gary shook out his blankets and crawled into them. In the moment before his eyes closed, he remembered the cattle had all worn a Double A brand, and the brands were fresh. That could easily be with a trail herd. But the Double A had been the spread that Mart Ray had mentioned.

It was raining when he rode out to the herd. "They ain't fussin'," Langer advised, "an' the rain's quiet enough. It should pass mighty easy. See you."

He drifted toward the camp, and Gary turned up his slicker collar and studied the herd as well as he could in the darkness. They were lying quietly. He was riding a gray, roped from the small remuda, and he let the horse amble placidly toward the far side of the meadow. A hundred yards beyond the meadow the bulk of the sloping hill that formed the opposite side of the valley showed blacker in the gloom. Occasionally there was a flash of heat lightening, but no thunder.

Slagle had taken him on because he needed hands, but none of them accepted him. He decided to sit tight in his saddle and see what developed. It could be plenty, for, unless he was mistaken, this was a stolen herd, and Slagle was a thief, as were the others. If this herd had come far and fast, he had come farther and faster, and with just as great a need. Now there was nothing behind him but trouble, and nothing before him but bleak years of drifting ahead of a reputation.

Up ahead was Mart Ray, and Ray was as much a friend as he had. Gunfighters are admired by many, respected by some, feared by all, and welcomed by none. His father had warned him of what to expect, warned him long ago before he himself had died in a gun battle. "You're right handy, Son," he had warned, "one of the fastest I ever seen, so don't let it be known. Don't ever draw a gun on a man in anger, and you'll live happy. Once you get the name of a gunfighter, you're on a lonesome trail, and there's only one ending."

So he had listened, and he had avoided trouble. Mart Ray knew that. Ray was himself a gunman. He had killed six men of whom Jim Gary knew, and no doubt there had been others. He and Mart had been riding together in Texas and then on a couple of trail drives, one all the way to Montana. He never really got close to Mart, but they had been partners after a fashion.

Ray had always been amused at his eagerness to avoid trouble, although he had no idea of the cause of it. "Well," he had said, "they sure cain't say like father, like son. From all I hear your pappy was an uncurried wolf, an' you fight shy of trouble. You run from it. If I didn't know you so well, I'd say you was yaller."

But Mart Ray had known him well, for it had been Jim who rode his horse down in front of a stampede to pick Ray off the ground, saving his life. They got free, but no more, and a thousand head of cattle stampeded over the ground where Ray had stood.

Then, a month before, down in the Big Bend country, trouble had come, and it was trouble he could not avoid. It braced him in a little Mexican *cantina* just over the river, and in the person of a dark, cat-like Mexican with small feet and dainty hands, but his guns were big enough and there was an unleashed devil in his eyes.

Jim Gary had been dancing with a Mexican girl, and the Mexican had jerked her from his arms and struck her across the face. Jim knocked him down, and the Mexican got up, his eyes fiendish. Without a word, the Mexican went for his gun, and for a frozen, awful instant Jim saw his future facing him, and then his own hand went down and he palmed his gun in a flashing, lightning draw that rapped out two shots. The Mexican, who had reached first, barely got his gun clear before he was dead. He died on his feet, and then fell.

In a haze of powder smoke and anguish, Jim Gary had wheeled and strode from the door, and behind him lay a dead and awful silence. It was not until two days later that he knew who and what he had killed. The lithe-bodied Mexican had been Miguel Sonoma, and he had been a legend along the border. A tough, dangerous man with a reputation as a killer.

Two nights later, a band of outlaws from over the border rode down upon Gary's little spread to avenge their former leader, and two of them died in the first blast of gunfire, a matter of handguns at point-blank

139

range. From the shelter of his cabin, Gary had fought them off for three days before the smoke from his burning barn attracted help. When the help had arrived, Jim Gary was a man with a name. Five dead men lay on the ground around the ranch yard and in the desert nearby. The wounded had been carried away. And the following morning, Jim turned his ranch over to the bank to sell and lit a shuck — away from Texas.

Of this, Mart Ray knew nothing. Half of Texas and all of New Mexico, or most of it, would lie behind him when Jim reached the banks of Salt Creek. Mart Ray was ramrodding the Double A, and he would have a job for him.

Jim Gary turned the horse and rode slowly back along the side of the herd. The cattle had taken their midnight stretch and, after standing around a bit, were lying down once more. The rain was falling, but softly, and Gary let the gray take his own time in skirting the herd.

The night was pitch dark. Only the horns of the cattle glistened with rain, and their bodies were darker blobs in the blackness of the night. Once, drawing up near the willows along the stream, Jim thought he detected a vague sound. He waited a moment, listening. On such a night nobody would be abroad who could help it, and it was unlikely that a mountain lion would be on the prowl, although possible.

He started on again, yet now his senses were alert, and his hand slid under his slicker and touched the butt of a .44. He was almost at the far end of the small herd

140

when a sudden flash of lightning revealed the hillside across the narrow valley.

Stark and clear, glistening with rain, sat a horseman. He was standing in his stirrups, and seemed amazingly tall, and in the glare of the flash his face was stark white, like the face of a fleshless skull.

Startled, Gary grunted and slid his gun into his hand, but all was darkness again, and, listen as he could, he heard no further sound. When the lightning flashed again, the hillside was empty and still. Uneasily he caught himself staring back over his shoulder into the darkness, and he watched his horse. The gray was standing, head up and ears erect, staring off toward the darkness near the hill. Riding warily, Gary started in that direction, but when he got there, he found nothing.

It was almost daylight when he rode up to the fire that had been kept up throughout the night, and, swinging down, he awakened Dirksen. The man sat up, startled. "Hey!" he exclaimed. "You forget to call me?"

Jim grinned at him. "Just figured I was already up and a good cook needed his sleep."

Jeeter stared at him. "You mean you rode for me? Say, you're all right!"

"Forget it." Gary stretched. "I had a quiet night, mostly."

Red Slagle was sitting up, awakened by their talk. "What do you mean . . . mostly?

Jim hesitated, feeling puzzled. "Why, to tell you the truth, I'm not sure whether I saw anything or not, but I sure thought I did. Anyway, it had me scared."

"What was it?" Slagle was pulling on his pants, but his eyes were serious. "A lion?"

"No, it was a man on a horse. A tall man with a dead-white face, like a skull." Gary shrugged sheepishly. "Makes me sound like a fool, but I figured for a moment that I'd seen a ghost."

Red Slagle was staring at him, and Jeeter's face was dead-white and his eyes were bulging. "A ghost?" he asked faintly. "Did you say a ghost?"

"Shucks" — Gary shrugged — "there ain't no such thing. Just some *hombre* on a big black horse, passing through in the night, that was all. But believe me, seeing him in the lightning up on that hill like I did, it sure was scary."

Tobe Langer was getting up, and he, too, looked bothered. Slagle came over to the fire and sat down, boots in hand. Reaching down, he pulled his sock around to get a hole away from his big toe, then he put his foot into the wet boot, and began to struggle with it.

"That horse, now," Langer asked carefully, "did it have a white star between the eyes?"

Gary was surprised. "Why, yes. Matter of fact, it did. You know him?"

Slagle let go of the boot and stomped his foot to settle it in the boot. "Yeah, feller we seen down the road a ways. Big black horse."

Slagle and Langer walked away from camp a ways, and stood talking together. Jeeter was worried. Jim could see that without half trying, and he studied the man thoughtfully. Jeeter Dirksen was a small man, quiet, but inclined to be nervous. He had neither the

142

strength nor the toughness of Slagle and Langer. If Gary learned anything about the cattle, it would be through his own investigation or from Jeeter. And he was growing more and more curious.

Yet if these were Double A cattle and had been stolen, why were they being driven toward the Double A Ranch, rather than away from it? He realized suddenly that he knew nothing at all about Red Slagle or his outfit, and it was time he made some inquiries.

"This Double A," he asked suddenly, "you been riding for them long?"

Dirksen glanced at him sharply and bent over his fire. "Not long," he said. "It's a Salt Creek outfit. Slagle's *segundo*."

"Believe I know your foreman," Gary suggested. "I think this was the outfit he said. *Hombre* name of Mart Ray. Ever hear of him?"

Jeeter turned sharply, slopping coffee over the rim of the cup. It hissed in the fire, and both the other men looked around at the camp. Jeeter handed the cup to Gary and studied him, searching his face. Then he admitted cautiously: "Yeah, Ray's the foreman. Ranch belongs to a syndicate out on the coast. You say you know him?"

"Uhn-huh. Used to ride with him." Langer and Slagle had walked back to the fire, and Dirksen poured coffee for them.

"Who was that you rode with?" Slagle asked.

"Your boss, Mart Ray."

Both men looked up sharply, then Slagle's face cleared and he smiled. "Say, that's why the name was familiar. You're *that* Jim Gary. Son of old Steve Gary. Yeah, Mart told us about you."

Langer chuckled suddenly. "You're the scary one, huh? The one who likes to keep out of trouble. Yeah, we heard about you."

The contempt in his tone stiffened Jim's back, and for an instant he was on the verge of a harsh retort. Then the memory of what lay behind him welled up within, and bitterly he kept his mouth shut. If he got on the prod and killed a man here, he would only have to drift farther. There was only one solution, and that was to avoid trouble. Yet, irritating as it was to be considered lacking in courage, Langer's remark let him know that the story of his fights had not preceded him.

"There's no call," he said after a minute, "to go around the country killing folks. If people would just get the idea they can get along without all that. Me, I don't believe in fighting."

Langer chuckled, but Slagle said nothing, and Dirksen glanced at him sympathetically.

All day the herd moved steadily west, but now Gary noticed a change, for the others were growing more watchful as the day progressed. Their eyes continued to search the surrounding hills, and they rode more warily approaching any bit of cover.

Once, when Jeeter rode near him, the little man glanced across the herd at the other riders and then said quietly: "That was no ghost you saw. Red rode up there on the hill, an' there was tracks, tracks of a mighty big black horse."

"Wonder why he didn't ride down to camp?" Jim speculated. "He sure enough saw the fire."

Dirksen grunted. "If that *hombre* was the one Red thinks it is, he sure didn't have no aim to ride down there."

Before Gary could question him further, Jeeter rode off after a stray and, cutting him back into the herd, rode on farther ahead. Jim dropped back to the drag, puzzling over this new angle. Who could the strange rider be? What did he want? Was he afraid of Slagle?

A big brindle steer was cutting wide of the herd, and Jim swung out to get him, but, dashing toward the stream, the steer floundered into the water and into quicksand. Almost at once, it was down, struggling madly, its eyes rolling.

Jim swung a loop and dropped it over the steer's horns. If he could give the steer a little help now, there was a chance he could get it out before it bogged in too deep.

He started the buckskin back toward more solid ground and with the pull on the rope and the struggling of the steer, he soon had it out on the bank of the stream. The weary animal stumbled and went down, and, shaking his loop loose, Gary swung his horse around to get the animal up. Something he saw on the flank made him swing down beside the steer. Curiously he bent over the brand.

It had been worked over. The Double A had been burned on over a Slash Four.

"Something wrong?"

The voice was cold and level, and Jim Gary started guiltily, turning. Then his eyes widened. "Mart! Well, for crying out in the nighttime. Am I glad to see you."

Ray stared. "For the luvva Pete, if it ain't Gary! Say, how did you get here? Don't tell me you're driving that herd up ahead?"

"That's right. Your outfit, ain't it? I hired on back down the line. This steer just got himself bogged down and I had a heck of a time getting him out. You seen Red and the boys?"

"Not yet. I swung wide. Get that steer on his feet and we'll join 'em."

Yet, as they rode back, despite Ray's affability, Gary was disturbed. Something here was very wrong. This was a Slash Four steer with the brand worked over to a Double A, the brand for which Ray was foreman. If these cattle were rustled, then Mart Ray was party to it, and so were Slagle, Langer, and Dirksen. And if he was caught with these men and cattle, so was he.

He replied to Ray's questions as well as he could, and briefly, aware that his friend was preoccupied and thinking of something else. Yet at the same time he was pleased that Ray asked him no questions about his reasons for leaving home.

Mart Ray rode up ahead and joined Slagle, and he could see the two men riding on together, deep in conversation. When they bedded down for the night, there had been no further chance to talk to him, and Gary was just as well satisfied, for there was much about this that he did not like. Nor was anything said about the midnight rider. When day broke, Mart Ray was gone. "Rode on to Salt Creek," Red said. "We'll see him there." He glanced at Jim, his eyes amused. "He said to keep you on, that you was a top hand."

Despite the compliment, Jim was nettled. What else had Ray told Slagle? His eyes narrowed. Whatever it was, he was not staying on. He was going to get shut of this outfit just as fast as he could. All he wanted was his time. Yet by midday he had not brought himself to ask for it.

Dirksen had grown increasingly silent, and he avoided Langer and Slagle. Watching him, Jim was puzzled by the man, but could find no reason for his behavior unless the man was frightened by something. Finally Jim pulled up alongside Jeeter.

The man glanced at him and shook his head. "I don't like this. Not even a little. She's too quiet."

Gary hesitated, waiting for the cowhand to continue, but he held his peace. Then, Gary said, speaking slowly: "It is mighty quiet, but I see nothing wrong with that. I'm not hunting trouble."

"Trouble," Jeeter said dryly, "comes sometimes whether you hunt it or not. If anything breaks around this herd, take my advice an' don't ask no questions. Just scatter dust out of here."

"Why are you warning me?" Gary asked.

Jeeter shrugged. "You seem like a right nice feller," he said quietly. "Shame for you to get rung in on somethin' as dirty as this when you had nothin' to do with it."

Despite his questions, Jeeter would say no more, and finally Gary dropped back to the drag. There was little dust because of the rains, but the drag was a rough deal, for the herd was tired and the cattle kept lagging back. Langer and Slagle, Jim observed, spent more time watching the hills than the cattle. Obviously both men were as jumpy as Dirksen and were expecting something. Toward dusk Red left the herd and rode up a cañon into the hills.

Slagle was still gone, and Jim was squatting by the fire watching Jeeter throw grub together when there was a sudden shot from the hills to the north.

Langer stopped his nervous pacing and faced the direction of the shot, his hand on his gun. Jim Gary got slowly to his feet, and he saw that Jeeter's knuckles gripping the frying pan were white and hard.

Langer was first to relax. "Red must have got him a turkey," he said. "Few around here, and he was sayin' earlier he'd sure like some."

Nevertheless, Gary noted that Langer kept back from the firelight and had his rifle near at hand. There was a sound of an approaching horse, and Langer slid his rifle across his knees, but it was Slagle. He swung down, glancing toward the big man. "Shot at a turkey an' missed." Then he added, looking right at Langer: "Nothin' to worry about now. This time for sure."

Dirksen got suddenly to his feet. "I'm quittin', Red. I don't like this a-tall, not none. I'm gettin' out."

Slagle's eyes were flat and ugly. "Sit down an' shut up, Jeeter," he said impatiently. "Tomorrow's our last day. We'll have a payday this side of Salt Creek, an' then, if you want to blow, why you can blow out of here."

Gary looked up. "I reckon you can have my time then, too," he said quietly. "I'm riding west for Pleasant Valley."

"You?" Langer snorted. "Pleasant Valley? You better stay somewhere where you can be took care of. They don't side-step trouble out there."

Gary felt something rise within him, but he controlled his anger with an effort. "I didn't ask you for any comment, Tobe," he said quietly. "I can take care of myself."

Langer sneered. "Why, you yaller skunk. I heard all about you. Just because your pappy was a fast man, you must think folks are skeered of you. You're yaller as saffron. You ain't duckin' trouble. You're just scared."

Gary was on his feet, his face white. "All you've got to do, Tobe, if you want to lose some teeth, is to stand up."

"What?" Langer leaped to his feet. "Why, you dirty . . ."

Jim Gary threw a roundhouse left. The punch was wide, but it came fast, and Langer was not expecting Jim to fight. Too late he tried to duck, but the fist caught him on the nose, smashing it and showering the front of his shirt with gore.

The big man was tough, and he sprang in, swinging with both hands. Gary stood his ground, and began to fire punches with both fists. For a full minute the two big men stood toe to toe and slugged wickedly, and then Gary deliberately gave ground. Overeager, Langer leaped after him, and Gary brought up a wicked right

149

that stood Tobe on his boot toes, and then a looping left that knocked him into the fire.

With a cry, he leaped from the flames, his shirt smoking. Ruthlessly Gary grabbed him by the shirt front and jerked him into a right hand to the stomach and then a right to the head, and shoving him away he split his ear with another looping left, smashing it like an overripe tomato. Langer went down in a heap.

Red Slagle had made no move to interfere, but his eyes were hard and curious as he stared up at Gary. "Now where," he said, "did Ray get the idea that you wouldn't fight?"

Gary spilled water from a canteen over his bloody knuckles. "Maybe he just figured wrong. Some folks don't like trouble. That doesn't mean they won't fight when they have to."

Langer pulled himself drunkenly to his feet and staggered toward the creek.

Red measured Jim with careful eyes. "What would you do," he asked suddenly, "if Langer reached for a gun?"

Gary turned his level green eyes toward Slagle. "Why, I reckon I'd have to kill him," he said matter-of-factly. "I hope he ain't so foolish."

Dawn broke cold and gray, and Jim Gary walked his horse up into the hills where he heard the shot the night before. He knew that, if Slagle saw him, he would be in trouble, but there was much he wanted to know.

Despite the light fall of rain the night before, there were still tracks. He followed those of Slagle's bay until he found where they joined those of a larger horse. Walking the buckskin warily, Jim followed the trail. It came to a sudden end.

A horse was sprawled in the clearing, shot through the head. A dozen feet away lay an old man, a tall old man, his sightless eyes staring toward the lowering skies, his arms flung wide. Jim bent over him and saw that he had been shot three times through the chest. Three times. And the wound lower down was an older wound, several days old, at least.

The horse wore a Slash Four brand. Things were beginning to make sense now. Going through the old man's pockets, Jim found a worn envelope containing some tallies of cattle, and the envelope was addressed to **Tom Blaze, Durango, Colo**.

Tom Blaze ... the Slash Four. Tom Blaze, the pioneer Kiowa-fighting cattleman who owned the Slash Four, one of the toughest outfits in the West. Why he had not connected the two, Jim could not imagine, but the fact remained that the Slash Four had struck no responsive chord in his thoughts until now. And Tom Blaze was dead.

Now it all fitted. The old Mother Hubbard saddle had been taken from Tom's horse, for this was the second time he had been shot. Earlier, perhaps when the cattle had been stolen, they had shot him and left him for dead, yet they had been unable to leave the saddle behind, for a saddle was two or three months' work for a cowhand and not to be lightly left behind.

They had been sure of themselves, too. Sure until Gary had seen Blaze, following them despite his wound. After that they had been worried, and Slagle must have sighted Blaze the afternoon before and then followed him and shot him down.

When the Slash Four found Tom Blaze dead, all hell would break loose. Dirksen knew that, and that was why he wanted out, but fast. And it was why Red Slagle and Tobe Langer had pushed so hard to get the cattle to Salt Creek, where they could be lost in larger herds or in the breaks of the hills around the Double A.

When he rode the buckskin down to the fire, the others were all up and moving around. Langer's face was swollen and there were two deep cuts, one on his cheek bone, the other over an eye. He was sullen and refused to look toward Gary.

Slagle stared at the buckskin suspiciously, noticing the wetness on his legs from riding in the high grass and brush.

Whatever the *segundo* had in mind he never got a chance to say. Jim Gary poured a cup of coffee, but held it in his left hand. "Red, I want my money. I'm taking out."

"Mind if I ask why?" Red's eyes were level and waiting.

Gary knew that Slagle was a gun hand, but the thought did not disturb him. While he avoided trouble, it was never in him to be afraid, nor did his own skill permit it. While he had matched gun speed with only one man, he had that sure confidence that comes from unerring marksmanship and speed developed from long practice.

152

"No, I don't mind. This morning I found Tom Blaze's body, right where you killed him yesterday afternoon. I know that Slash Four outfit, and I don't want to be any part of this bunch when they catch up to you."

His frankness left Slagle uncertain. He had been prepared for evasion. This was not only sincerity, but it left Slagle unsure as to Gary's actual stand. From his words Slagle assumed Gary was leaving from dislike of fight rather than dislike of rustling.

"You stick with us, Jim," he said. "You're a good man, like Mart said. That Slash Four outfit won't get wise, and there'll be a nice split on this cattle deal."

"I want no part of it," Jim replied shortly. "I'm out. Let me have my money."

"I ain't got it," Red said simply. "Ray pays us all off. I carry no money around. Come on, Jim, lend us a hand. We've only today, then we'll be at the head of Salt Creek Wash and get paid off."

Gary hesitated. He did need the money, for he was broke and would need grub before he could go on west. Since he had come this far, another day would scarcely matter. "All right, I'll finish the drive."

Nothing more was said, and within the hour they moved out. Yet Gary was restless and worried. He could feel the tenseness in the others and knew they, too, were disturbed. There was no sign of Mart Ray, who should be meeting them soon.

To make matters worse, the cattle were growing restive. The short drives had given them time to recover some of their energy, and several of them, led by one

153

big red steer, kept breaking for the brush. It was hot, miserable work. The clouds still hung low, threatening rain, but the air was sultry.

Jim Gary started the day with the lean gray horse he had ridden before, but by mid-afternoon he had exchanged the worn-out animal for his own buckskin. Sweat streamed down his body under his shirt, and he worked hard, harrying the irritable animals down the trail that now was lined with piñon and juniper, with a sprinkling of huge boulders. Ahead, a wide cañon opened, and not far beyond would be the spot where he expected to find Ray with the pay-off money.

The big red steer suddenly made another bolt for the brush, and the buckskin unwound so fast that it almost unseated Gary. He swore softly and let the horse take him after the steer and cut it back to the herd. As it swung back, he glanced up to see Langer and Red Slagle vanishing into the brush. Where Dirksen was he could not guess until he heard a wild yell.

Swinging around, he saw a dozen hard-riding horsemen cutting down from the brush on both sides, and a glance told him that flight was useless. Nevertheless, Jeeter Dirksen tried it.

Slamming the spurs into his bronco, Dirksen lunged for the brush in the direction taken by Slagle and Langer, but he had made no more than a dozen yards when a rattle of gunfire smashed him from the saddle. His slender body hit the ground rolling, flopped over one last time, and lay, sprawled and sightless, under the low gray clouds.

Gary rested his hands on his saddle horn and stared gloomily at the strange little man, so badly miscast in this outlaw venture. Then horsemen closed in around him; his six-guns were jerked from their holsters and his rifle from its scabbard.

"What's the matter with you?" The voice was harsh. "Won't that horse of yours run?"

Jim looked up into a pair of cold gray eyes in a leather-like face. A neat gray mustache showed above a firm-lipped mouth. Jim Gary smiled, although he had never felt less like it in his life. The horsemen surrounded him, and their guns were ready. "Never was much of a hand to run," Jim said, "and I've done nothing to run for."

"You call murderin' my brother nothin'? You call stealin' cattle nothin'? Sorry, friend, we don't see things alike. I call it hangin'."

"So would I, only I haven't done those things. I hired onto this outfit back down the line. Forty bucks to the head of Salt Creek Wash . . . and they ain't paid me."

"You'll get paid!" The speaker was a lean, hard-faced young man. "With a rope!"

Another rider, a girl, pushed a horse through the circle. "Who is this man, Uncle Dan? Why didn't he try to get away?"

"Says he's just a hired hand," Uncle Dan commented.

"That's probably what that dead man would have said, too!" the lean cowpuncher said. "Let me an' the boys have him under that cottonwood we seen. It had nice strong limbs."

Gary had turned his head to look at the girl. Uncle Dan would be Dan Blaze, and this must be the daughter of the murdered man. She was tall and slim, but rounded of limb and undeniably attractive, with color in her cheeks and a few scattered freckles over her nose. Her eyes were hazel and now looked hard and stormy.

"Did you folks find Tom Blaze's body?" he asked. "They left him back yonder." Lifting a hand carefully to his shirt pocket, he drew out the envelope and tally sheets. "These were his."

"What more do you need?" the lean cowpuncher demanded. He pushed his horse against Jim's and grabbed at the buckskin's bridle. "Come on, boys!"

"Take it easy, Jerry!" Dan Blaze said sharply. "When I want him hung, I'll say so." His eyes shifted back to Jim. "You're a mighty cool customer," he said. "If your story's straight, what are you doing with these?"

As briefly as possible, Jim explained the whole situation and ended by saying: "What could I do? I still had forty bucks coming, and I did my work, so I aim to collect. You say there were three men with the herd? And the two who got away were Tobe Langer and Red Slagle?"

"That's right," Jim hesitated over Mart Ray, and then said no more.

Blaze was staring at the herd, and now he looked at Jim. "Why were these cattle branded Double A? That's a straight outfit. You know anything about that?"

Gary hesitated. Much as he had reason to believe Ray was not only one of these men but their leader, he hated to betray him. "Not much. I don't know any of these outfits. I'm a Texas man."

Blaze smiled wryly. "You sound it. What's your handle?"

"Jim Gary."

The cowpuncher named Jerry started as if struck. "Jim Gary?" he gasped, his voice incredulous. "The one who killed Sonoma?"

"Yeah, I reckon."

Now they were all staring at him with new interest, for the two fights he had were ample to start his name growing a legend on the plains and desert. These cowpunchers had heard of him, probably from some grubline rider or drifting cowpuncher.

"Jim Gary," Blaze mused. "We've heard about you. Old Steve's son, aren't you? I knew Steve."

Jim looked up, his eyes cold. "My father," he said grimly, "was a mighty good man."

Dan Blaze's eyes warmed a little. "You're right. He was."

"What of it?" Jerry demanded sullenly. "The man's a killer. We know that. We found him with the cattle. We found him with some of Tom's stuff on him. What more do you want?"

The girl spoke suddenly. "There was another rider, one who joined you and then rode away. Who was he?"

There it was, and Jim suddenly knew he would not lie. "Mart Ray," he said quietly, "of the Double A."

"That's a lie!" The girl flashed back. "What are you saying?"

"You got any proof of that?" Jerry demanded hotly. "You're talkin' about a friend of our'n."

"He was a friend of mine, too." Gary explained about Mart Ray. "Why don't you turn me loose?" he suggested then. "I'll go get Ray and bring him to you. Chances are Slagle and Tobe will be with him."

"You'll get him?" Jerry snorted. "That's a good one, that is."

"Tie him," Dan Blaze said suddenly. "We'll go into Salt Creek."

Riding behind Dan Blaze and his niece, who he heard them call Kitty, Jim Gary was suddenly aware, almost for the first time, of the danger he was in. The fact that it had been averted for the moment was small consolation, for these were hard, desperate men, and one of their number, perhaps more, had been slain.

Fear was something strange to him, and, while he had known danger, it had passed over him, leaving him almost untouched. This situation conveyed only a sense of unreality, and until now the idea that he might really be in danger scarcely seemed credible. Listening to these men, his mind changed about that. He realized belatedly that he was in the greatest danger of his life. If he had none of their talk to warn him, the mute evidence of Jeeter's body was enough. And Jeeter had died yelling to him, trying to give him a warning so he might escape.

Now fear rode with him, a cold, clammy fear that stiffened his fingers and left his mouth dry and his stomach empty. Even the sight of the scattered buildings of the town of Salt Creek did not help, and, when they rode up the street, the red of embarrassment crept up his neck at the shame of being led into the town, his hands tied behind him, like a cheap rustler.

Mart Ray was sitting on the steps, and he shoved his hat back and got to his feet. Beside him was Red Slagle. There was no sign of Tobe Langer. "Howdy, Dan! What did you catch? A hoss thief?" Ray's voice was genial, his eyes bland. "Looks like a big party for such a small catch."

Blaze reined in his horse and stopped the little cavalcade. His eyes went from Mart to Slagle. "How long you been here, Red?" he demanded.

"Me?" Slagle was innocent. "No more'n about fifteen minutes, maybe twenty. Just rode in from the Double A. Somethin' wrong?"

Blaze turned his cold eyes on Jim Gary, and then looked back to Ray. "We found a herd of Slash Four cattle east of here, Mart. They were wearin' a Double A brand worked over our Slash Four. How do you explain it?"

Ray shrugged. "I don't," he said simply. "How does that *hombre* you got with you explain it?"

Kitty Blaze spoke up quickly: "Mart, did you ever see this man before? Did you?"

Ray stared at Gary. "Not that I recall," he said seriously. "He sure don't look familiar to me."

"Blaze," Gary said suddenly, "if you'll turn my hands loose and give me a gun, I can settle this in three minutes. I can prove he's a liar. I can prove that he does know me and that I know him."

"There's nothin' you can prove with a gun you can't prove without it," Blaze said flatly. "Whatever you know, spill it. Else you're gettin' your neck stretched. I'm tired of this fussin' around."

Jim Gary kneed his horse forward. His eyes were hot and angry. "Mart," he said, "I always suspected there was a streak of coyote in you, but I never knew you'd be this low-down. I don't like to remind anybody of what I did for him, but I recall a stampede I hauled you out of. Are you going to talk?"

Ray shook his head, smiling. "This is a lot of trouble, Dan. Take him away and stretch his neck before I get sore and plug him."

"You'd be afraid to meet me with a gun, Mart. You always were afraid," Jim taunted. "That's why you left Red and Tobe with the cattle. You wanted the profit but none of the trouble. Well, you've got trouble now. If I had a gun, I'd see you eat dirt."

Mart Ray's face was ugly. "Shut up, you fool! You call me yellow? Why, everybody knows you're yellow as . . ." He caught himself abruptly, his face paling under the tan.

"What was that, Ray?" Dan Blaze's face had sharpened. "Everybody knows what about him? If you've never seen him before, how could you say everybody calls him yellow?"

Ray shrugged. "Just talkin' too fast, that's all!" He turned and stepped up on the sidewalk. "He's your man. You settle your own war." Ray turned to go, but Jim yelled at him, and Ray wheeled.

"Mart, if I don't know you, how do I know you've got a white scar down your right side, a scar made by a steer's hoof?"

Ray laughed, but it was a strained laugh. He looked trapped now, and he took an involuntary step backward. "That's silly," he scoffed. "I've no such scar."

"Why not take off your shirt?" Jerry said suddenly. "That will only take a minute." The lean-jawed cowhand's face was suddenly hard. "I think I remember you having such a scar, from one time I seen you swimmin' in the San Juan. Take off your shirt an' let's see!"

Mart Ray backed up another step, his face sharp and cold. "I'll be damned if I take off my shirt in the street for any low-down rustler," he snapped. "This here nonsense has gone far enough."

"Loose my hands," Jim pleaded in a whisper. "I'll take his shirt off."

Kitty stared at him. Her face was white and strained, but in her eyes he now saw a shadow of doubt. Yet it was Jerry who acted suddenly, jerking him around before anyone realized what he had done and severing the bonds with a razor-sharp knife and jerking the ropes from his hands. With almost the same gesture, he slammed guns in Gary's holsters. "All right. Maybe I'm crazy," he snapped. "But go to it."

The whole action had taken less than a minute, and Mart Ray had turned his back and started away while Blaze waited in indecision. It was Red Slagle who saw Jim Gary hit the ground. "Boss!" he yelled. His voice was suddenly sharp with panic. "Look out!"

Ray wheeled, and, when he saw Gary coming toward him, chafing his wrists, he stood still, momentarily dumbfounded. Then he laughed. "All right, yellow. You're askin' for it. This is one bunch of trouble you can't duck. You've ducked your last fight."

Furious, he failed to realize the import of his words, and he dropped into a half crouch, his hands ready above his gun butts. It was Jerry who shook him, Jerry who made the casual remark that jerked Mart Ray to realization of what he was facing.

"Looks like whatever Ray knows about him, he sure ain't heard about Jim Gary killin' Miguel Sonoma."

Mart Ray was staggered. "Sonoma?" he gasped. "You killed Sonoma?"

Jim Gary was facing him now. Some of the numbness was gone from his hands, and something cold and terrible was welling up within him. He had ridden beside this man, shared food with him, worked with him, and now the man had tricked and betrayed him. "Yes, Mart, I killed Sonoma. I ain't afraid. I never was. I just don't like trouble."

Ray's tongue touched his lips and his eyes narrowed to slits. He sank a little deeper into the crouch, and men drew away to the sides of the street. Scarcely twenty feet apart, the two faced each other. "Take off your shirt, Ray. Take if off and show them. Reach up slow and unbutton it. You take it off yourself, or I'll take it off your body."

"Go to blazes!" Ray's voice was hoarse and strange. Then, with incredible swiftness, his hands dropped for his guns.

162

In the hot, dusty stillness of the afternoon street, all was deathly still. Somewhere a baby cried, and a foot shifted on the boardwalk. For what seemed an age, all movement seemed frozen and still as the two men in the street faced each other.

Kitty Blaze, her eyes wide with horror, seemed caught in that same breathless time-frozen hush. The hands of the men were moving with flashing speed, but at that instant everything seemed to move hauntingly slow. She saw Mart Ray's gun swing up; she saw the killing eagerness in his face, his lips thinned and white, his eyes blazing. And she saw the stranger, Jim Gary, tall, lithe, and strong, his dark face passionless, yet somehow ruthless. And she saw his lean brown hand flash in a blur of movement, saw flame leap from the black muzzles of his guns, and saw Mart Ray smashed back, back, back! She saw his body flung sideways into the hitching rail, saw a horse rear, his lashing hoofs within inches of the man. She saw the gun blaze again from the ground, and a leap of dust from the stranger's shoulder, and she saw Gary move coolly aside to bring his guns better to bear upon the man who was now struggling up. As in a kind of daze, she saw Jim Gary holding his fire, letting Ray get to his feet. In that stark, incredible instant, she saw him move his lips and she heard the words, as they all heard them in the silence of the street. "I'm sorry, Mart. You shouldn't have played it this way. I'd rather it had been the stampede."

And when Ray's guns swung up, his shirt was bloody, his face twisted in a sort of leer torn into his cheek by a bullet, and his eyes were fiendish. The guns

163

came up, and even as they came level, red flame stabbed from the muzzles of Gary's guns and Ray's body jerked, dust sprang from his shirt's back, and he staggered back and sat down on the edge of the walk, and then, as though taken with a severe pain in the groin, he rolled over into the street and sprawled out flat. Somewhere thunder rolled.

For a long moment, the street was motionless. Then somebody said: "We better get inside. She's rainin'."

Jerry swung from his horse and in a couple of strides was beside the fallen man. Ripping back the shirt, he exposed the side, scarred by a steer's hoof.

Dan Blaze jerked around. "Slagle!" he yelled. "Where's Red Slagle! Get him!"

"Here." Slagle was sitting against the building, gripping a bloody hand. "I caught a slug. I got behind Ray." He looked up at Blaze. "Gary's right. He's straight as a string. It was Ray's idea to ring him in and use him as the goat after he found him with us."

Dan Blaze knelt beside him. "Who killed my brother?" he demanded. "Was it you or Ray?"

"Ray shot him first. I finished it. I went huntin' him an' he busted out of the brush. He had a stick he'd carried for walkin' an' I mistook it for a gun."

"What about Langer?" Gary demanded. "Where is he?"

Red grinned, a hard, cold grin. "He lit a shuck. That whuppin' you gave him took somethin' out of him. Once he started to run, he didn't stop, not even for his money." He dug into his pocket. "That reminds me. Here's the forty bucks you earned." Jim Gary took the

164

money, surprised speechless. Slagle struggled erect. Gary's expression seemed to irritate him. "Well, you earned it, didn't you? An' I hired you, didn't I? Well, I never gypped no man out of honest wages yet. Anyway," he added wryly, "by the looks of that rope I don't reckon I'll need it. Luck to you, kid." He grinned. "Stay out of trouble."

Thunder rumbled again, and rain poured into the street, a driving, pounding rain that would start the washes running and bring the grass to life again, green and waving for the grazing cattle, moving west, moving north.

Acknowledgments

"His Brother's Debt" under the byline Jim Mayo first appeared in *Giant Western* (4/50). Copyright © 1950 by Best Publications, Inc. Copyright not renewed.

"A Strong Land Growing" first appeared in *Texas Rangers* (1/55). Copyright © 1955 by Better Publications, Inc. Copyright not renewed.

"Lit a Shuck for Texas" first appeared in *Thrilling Western* (5/48). Copyright © 1948 by Standard Magazines, Inc. Copyright not renewed.

"The Nester and the Paiute" first appeared in *Exciting Western* (7/48). Copyright © 1948 by Better Publications, Inc. Copyright not renewed.

"Barney Takes a Hand" first appeared in *Thrilling Western* (10/46). Copyright © 1946 by Standard Magazines, Inc. Copyright not renewed.

"Man Riding West" under the byline Jim Mayo first appeared in *West* (1/50). Copyright © 1949 by Better Publications, Inc. Copyright not renewed.

166

About the Editor

Jon Tuska is the author of numerous books about the American West as well as editor of several short story collections, *Billy the Kid : His Life and Legend* (Greenwood Press, 1994) and *The Western Story: A Chronological Treasury* (University of Nebraska Press, 1995) among them. Together with his wife Vicki Piekarski, Tuska co-founded Golden West Literary Agency that primarily represents authors of Western fiction and Western Americana. They edit and co-publish thirty titles a year in two prestigious series of new Western novels and story collections, the Five Star Westerns and the Circle Ⓥ Westerns. They also co-edited the *Encyclopedia of Frontier and Western Fiction* (McGraw-Hill, 1983), *The Max Brand Companion* (Greenwood Press, 1996), *The Morrow Anthology of Great Western Short Stories* (Morrow, 1997), and *The Gunsmoke Corral of Great Western Stories* (Gunsmoke, 2013), available in book form and a full-length audio version from AudioGO.